NEW BLOOD

New Blood

(Blood Rights, Book Eight)

K. B. Thorne

*To all the unconventional people out there, living their lives
as themselves. Live and love well.*

In Somnis Veritas

I hate dreaming.

No matter how much I hate it, though, I keep doing it. Every night, my subconscious plunges me into an ephemeral world based off memories of places I can never see again, and people I can never talk to again. I visit the seascapes of one of the more remote fae realms, knowing that I have been exiled forever from those places.

Tonight is no different. I'm sitting on a beach of pure black sand, looking out over blue-green waters that roll in and away from the shore at the same lazy pace as all the eternal beings that call this place home. I know I'm dreaming, because fae dreams are always lucid, but that doesn't mean I like it.

It doesn't take me long to realize, however, that tonight is different. There is something different, but I don't know what it is. My 'Spidey sense' goes off as I start looking around, leaving the sad fae behind and becoming the me I am in the non-dreaming world.

By the way, my name is Posey Kai, and I work for the Federal Bureau of Investigation.

My eyes roam the beach and soon I see the source of the disturbance. There is a person, and I know instantly that my imagination didn't create them. This is an actual person whose subconscious has somehow joined my dream, which tells me instantly that they aren't human either. Humans don't have that power, unless they're psychic and even then, it's only the dreams of other humans. My dreams are shielded by nature, though not impervious.

Obviously.

He's walking toward me, and I stand to meet him. As he draws near, he stops and looks at me with surprise. Most people do, at least in real life. I'm not very tall, and my eyes are unnaturally large compared to humans. My hair and eyes are both close to teal in color, and that has nothing to do with dyes or contacts. It's my heritage, but thanks to Cameron's Law, I can be fae and legally so. (Not that I like telling people I'm fae. It invites too many questions that I don't want to answer.)

After recovering from his initial shock, he comes up to me. I stand and wait for him.

"This isn't my dream," he says.

He's pretty, I can't deny that. Tall and lean, with an almost amber shade to those brown eyes and coffee-brown hair, long and pulled back in a ponytail. He's also got an accent: French.

"No, it's not," I reply plainly. "How did you get here?"

He frowns and looks out over my seascape. "I'm not entirely sure. I dream all the time and of course I can see the dreams of others, like bubbles that I spend my time floating between, but I've never been pulled into one. You pulled me in."

My teal brows lift. "Not by choice. I've never pulled anyone into a dream before, and I've been dreaming for a long time."

"It's beautiful," he says, turning back to me.

"It is." I pause. "By this point, either introduce yourself or leave."

My curtness seems to amuse him, and he smiles. Holding his hand out, he says, "I'm Adrien."

I look at his hand and then take it. "Posey."

He tilts his head. "I've never met anyone with that name before."

"First time for everything," I say.

It's not like I usually strike up conversations with strangers, but this is the dreamscape, and that offers a certain amount of protection. He can't hurt me, so I'm free to let my curiosity roam, and I'm very curious.

He smiles at me and this time, it's dazzling. It's broad and open, and it nearly knocks me off my feet. Swallowing hard, I turn and start walking. I have to look away from him. As I walk, though, I can feel him fall in line beside me. His long legs have to take smaller steps than he's used to, I'm sure, to keep up with my diminutive stature.

"What is this place?" he asks.

"It's called the Sea of Forever," I reply. For some reason, it seems easier to talk to someone about these things in a dream than in real life. "It belongs to the fae realm of Dalora."

From my peripheral vision, I can see his brows go up. "So, you're fae."

I smile a little and steal a sidelong glance. "I am. I grew up there."

His eyes narrow thoughtfully, and I look forward again, keeping an eye on where my feet go in the loose sand. "If you were still there, I would not be in your dream."

"No," I agreed. "I live on Earth now."

"So do I," he said. "But then, I always have."

I look at him again. "You're not human."

He smiles wryly. "I used to be."

Well, that answers that, and it explains his presence in my dream. "Ah, so you're a vampire." I know that the coma-like sleep vampires go into during the daylight hours puts them into an interesting state. Most vampires don't remember the dreams they have during that time, but a rare few do. Then again, he might not remember this at all when he woke, and there was something freeing about that. I could say anything, and he wouldn't remember.

Not like we'll ever see one another again anyways.

"I am," he agrees.

"From France," I add.

He looks at me with surprise for a moment, then laughs. "The accent."

I smile at him. "The accent."

Adrien shrugs, and we keep walking. There is something...pleasant about this. I suppose I haven't really gotten to know anyone, outside of work, for a long time. In fact, I don't know that I can recall the last person I met and introduced myself to who wasn't associated with my work.

"So, what brings a fae to live on Earth?" he asks. It's the natural question, I suppose, and the one I want to answer least.

"To be honest, I don't like to talk about it," I tell him plainly, with an apologetic smile.

He seems to accept this easily. Perhaps he has skeletons in his closet too. Honestly, I've rarely met a vampire who doesn't. Well, I've rarely met a living being—or not living being—who doesn't, but not everyone accepts it too well of others. They want to keep their demons private but are offended when others try to do the same.

"So, what do you do on Earth, then?" he asks instead and gives me that blinding smile.

My breath is momentarily sucked out of my body, and I swallow against my dry throat before I can reply. "I'm a cop," I say. "I work for the FBI."

He nods. "So you are in the States, then. You can be as you are."

I smile and nod. "I can. It says 'fae' on all of my applications, although I don't always tell people about it if I think they don't need to know."

For a moment, my mind wanders. Cameron's Law has made preternatural beings legal citizens in the United States, but the rest of the world hasn't followed suit. Most of the European Union has, though, or are in the process of it. I try to recall about France.

"France should be the same soon," I say.

"Perhaps so," he agrees. "It seems that it was no small pill for the world to swallow, when the US began their law."

"It was no small pill for the US to swallow either," I point out.

He laughs. "Quite so. But still, if something like this is to take place, it would be amongst you brash Americans, wouldn't it?" I turn my head to look at him, and his eyes are glittering with mirth. I can't help but smile.

After a few moments of companionable silence, I ask, "You really don't have any idea how you ended up in my dream?"

Adrien shakes his head. "I do not. It has never happened before. Perhaps I was just not paying enough attention and you have a strong dream field..." He trails off uncertainly. "But the view is quite lovely, so I'm not going to complain."

I look at him, about to agree that the sea is beautiful, but then I realize he's looking right at me and doesn't mean the water at all. I'm not actually accustomed to being flirted with, so I almost blush and then almost stumble. I manage to avoid both, but barely. I hold his eyes for a few moments more and then turn my attention forward again.

There's a beeping noise that makes him frown and stop, looking around. It takes me a moment to realize what it is...

"I'm sorry," I tell him with a faint smile. "I've got to g—"

☾○☽

Groaning, I snake my hand out from under the blankets and smack my alarm clock until it stops making that infernal racket.

Once there is silence, I push the blanket away from my head and roll onto my back. My ceiling is pale blue. Everything in my apartment is some shade of blue, gray, or green. I can't help but think back to that dream, though. I'd had a vampire invade my subconscious realm, but I couldn't find it in me to be bothered. He had seemed…nice.

It's five o'clock in the evening. I work the night shift, because my partner Jackson and I handle the preternatural cases and those happen predominantly at night. Slipping out of bed, I take a shower. I take a lot of showers. I need the water. It isn't unheard of for me to shower before I go to work and after I get home. I think my water bill is the highest bill I have behind rent, but we do what we must to remain sane, right?

After showering and getting dressed, I eat dinner (breakfast?). I run some errands, because I know I'm not going to want to buy laundry detergent and cereal at three or four in the morning. Feeling nice for some reason, I buy a couple coffees on my way to the office.

When I pull into my parking space in front of the FBI preternatural satellite office in New London, hidden away in a building that doesn't look like what it is in the historical-feeling seaside downtown, I see that Jackson is already there but hasn't gone in yet. He's standing beside his car with his girlfriend, so I loiter in my own vehicle pretending to be busy until I hear a car door shut and know she's driven away.

It's not that I'm uncomfortable, but I like to afford privacy when I can. It seems polite.

Grabbing up the coffees and my purse, I step out and

see him walking to the door. He turns when he hears me and smiles.

"Is that for me?" he asks, nodding at the tray.

"No, it's for my other partner. He's cuter." I smile back and walk past him into the building.

The outside may be designed to blend in with the look of the town around it, but the inside is all the sterile efficiency one would expect from a law enforcement office: obnoxious fluorescent lighting, off-white tile, and eggshell-colored walls. (Then again, I've seen eggs and no egg I've ever seen has been 'eggshell' color.)

I hand him one of the Styrofoam cups, and we pass through the door into our specific office. For some reason, I find myself drifting back to my dreamscape and the man, Adrien...

"You're famous." Jackson grins as he pulls out the folded paper from under his arm and drops it on my desk. I don't know what he's up to until I look at it and see the *Adelheid Chronicle*, and that the side bar has...

Me.

Oh, hell.

I had completely forgotten about that damn interview. Our section lead had pressured me into it, saying I was a good 'face' for the bureau's preternatural arm (read: more attractive than Jackson, so long as it was black and white) and he wanted the good press. Since I didn't do undercover work, it happened. Now I'm staring at an article about myself and want to dig a hole under the building.

"Take that thing away," I mutter, wondering why I let myself get talked into it. Oh, right, because it was my boss and I didn't really have a choice.

Jackson chuckles at my distress but picks up the paper and stuffs it in his own desk drawer. We settle into our start-of-shift routine, and I field a few basic phone calls, but my brain is not settled on it. I keep thinking about my dream. No, I keep thinking about Adrien—the man or the mystery of his appearance in my dreamscape, I don't know. Am I behaving like a high school kid or intrigued by a puzzle? I'm not sure.

The phone rings again. I love music and lyrical things, so I hate the ringing of the telephone. I answer it, "Kai."

"Is this Posey Kai?"

"Yes. May I ask who this is?" I ask, not thinking much about it.

There's a long pause. "Special Agent Posey Kai, who was interviewed in the *Chronicle*?"

This draws my attention more closely, and I sigh. I knew that interview was a bad idea. "Yes, can I help you?"

"What are you?"

That's perhaps as common a question since legalization as 'what do you do' used to be, but there's something about the tone that sends an unnerving chill down my spine. I start analyzing. The voice sounds to be a male. I estimate between twenty and thirty, and I'm better at auditory clues than visual ones. There's a tone to his speaking that sounds like he's stiff, trying to cover up the regular sound of his voice and speech patterns. Maybe an accent.

"What is your business?" I keep my tone as bland and professional as possible, but Jackson has picked up on it and is frowning at me.

The caller doesn't reply, but it's many long seconds before the line is cut. I frown and hang up the phone.

"It begins," I say, knowing how dark I sound, but I can't help it. I relay to him the contents of the brief conversation and my impressions.

"Keep track of any of those you get and if they get worse, you better damn well tell me," he states. Nothing threatening had actually been said, so there isn't much else to be done on the matter. I do take notes on it, however. And I smile at

Jackson for his protective nature. He seems to have taken the role of big brother to me. He doesn't know much about me, but he knows more than most. He knows I don't have anyone here.

The rest of the day passes like most days, which is actually fairly boring. Television makes it look far more exciting all the time than it actually is.

I go home. It's about twenty minutes past three in the morning when I enter my apartment and lock the door behind me. I rub the back of my head and pull my hair loose from the tight braid I keep it in for work. I make myself something to eat and a cup of tea. I check my personal email, which I don't do at work, then I change for bed and read for a while to unwind so I can go to sleep. And I realize that I'm looking forward to it, wondering if I won't be alone in my dreams.

☾O☽

It seems to take forever for me to fall asleep, and when I finally do, I realize that my dreamscape has changed. It's... the French countryside, if I'm not mistaken. I could be, as I've only been there once. It is certainly enough to keep me looking at the scenery rather than anything else. I don't even turn until I hear someone clearing their throat and turn to see my visitor from last night.

"Your doing?" I ask, gesturing around me.

"Yes," he says with an almost sheepish expression. "I am not entirely sure how, when this is your dream, but this is where I frequent. It is not far from where I grew up, although this is how I looked in my day. It's different now."

"Is it rude to ask a vampire how old they are?" I ask, hoping my smile will be enough to make it not be even if it is.

He laughs. "I don't know what's in fashion for vampires these days." Pausing, his face loses expression as he thinks of something. "I was born in the seventeen-seventies. I actually almost forget the particular year."

That catches my attention. I tilt my head. "You were born before the French Revolution."

Turning his head, he looks at me with a somber expression as he nods. "I was."

I look over his face for a long moment. "You had to have been turned young," I state.

"Not even twenty," he replies and then laughs ruefully. "I don't normally like talking about this, but…"

"Something about it being a dream makes it easier?" I finish for him.

"Yes." He smiles, and I wonder where my sunglasses are. I feel faint, which I tell myself is stupid but there it is. "Did you remember me when you woke?"

I smile. "I did. Did you remember me?"

Something dark fills his eyes, but just for a moment. "Yes, I did. I'm not sure I could ever not remember now."

The statement could mean anything, but there is something in his tone that makes me think it's a compliment, and I feel a little shy. I can't remember the last time someone flirted with me who I actually was interested in flirting with. But it feels safe here, in a way that I didn't realize until now felt unsafe in the world.

We are walking and start moving down the hill. He's pointing out things about it, animals and plants, with an eye unlike anyone's I have ever known. I know those who look at things with the keen eye of the detective, but he sees…beauty everywhere.

"Are you some kind of artist?" I finally ask.

He stops walking so suddenly that I almost fall down a hill trying to stop as well and turn back to him. His expression is curious. It's not upset, precisely, but it's not *not* upset either.

"How did you know that?" he asks.

"The way you talk about things," I tell him. "Remember, I'm a cop. I can figure things out. You see beauty in everything, little things that I never would have considered."

That odd expression takes on an edge that's almost... stricken. I don't even know this man, but it seems to cut me as well. I step closer and hold his gaze. "I didn't mean to say anything to offend you," I say quietly, feeling my brows knit with uncertainty.

He swallows visibly with a slow shake of his head. "It's... No, I'm sorry. You just startled me, is all." Adrien smiles, but it's obviously forced and not as bright. "Yes, I was a painter."

"You *were* a painter?" It's impossible to miss the past tense. "You don't paint anymore?"

"No, I don't," he says, bowing his head and walking again.

I catch myself being guilty of what I chastise others for: being annoyed when someone won't tell me about their past, when I do the same thing all the time. Sighing, I hurry to catch up and keep walking with him down the hill. I don't say anything, because I don't really know what to say. Neither of us say anything for a while. Apparently, I've made him uncomfortable and he doesn't want to talk anymore.

Normally, the silence doesn't bother me. Right now, it does.

"So, you still live in France, right?" I ask, because I have to talk.

"I do, yes," he says. There is a war on his face trying to overcome his previous agitation, and I wonder if he's the worst vampire I've ever met at hiding his feelings, or if it's an effect of being on the dreamscape. "I have never lived anywhere else. You could say that I am...a part of the land." He laughs, but it's a humorless sound—almost chillingly so. I fight a shiver along my skin, as sounds have particular strength for me.

I want to ask, I want to ask very badly, but Adrien is…a new friend? I'm not sure what to call him, in these unique circumstances, but I do know that he's not a suspect in my interrogation room so it's rude to push. It makes my skin itch to not ask.

"After I…left Dalora," I begin, because apparently in the dreamscape, I need to hear someone talking, "I ended up in Japan. It's where the only portal from Dalora exists, and I can tell you that I stood out a little. I couldn't speak Japanese, but someone said to me in English that I looked like an anime character." I chuckle at the memory. "Glamour isn't my strong suit, but I was able to use enough to blend in until I was able to get to America."

"How did you become a cop?" he asks, seeming to relax now that the conversation has moved off him.

"It wasn't my original plan," I admit, "but I made a friend once I was in the States and she wanted to be a cop. It…felt right, to follow her." I don't tell him why that is, even though I know the reason. "After Cameron's Law, I was able to come out of the paranormal closet and being preternatural was an asset. I was able to join the FBI and became part of the offshoot that deals with the weird stuff. My partner is a pyrokinetic."

Adrien tilts his head. I see the uncertainty in his gaze.

I smile. "He's a human psychic and can play with fire. Don't piss him off. I saw him smack a table once and leave a burnt wooden handprint behind."

His eyes widen. "I've heard of them, obviously, but have never met a fire witch."

His antiquated term almost makes me giggle. I almost make a joke about not letting Jackson hear him call him that, but then I realize that Jackson will never hear him call anyone anything. Jackson will never meet him. The realization is startlingly a little sad. I don't know what it is, but there's something about him.

How is it I finally really connect with someone and I only meet him in a damn dream?

"You suddenly looked an ocean away," he says, and I blink. It takes me a moment to catch the small, crooked smile of his humor.

I laugh. "I suppose I am," I reply with levity, and his smile grows.

The silence as we walk this time is more comfortable than before. He asks me questions about my job, which I'm happy to answer. Nothing he asks is anything I have to keep secret. Some of his questions are surprising, though, and things I would think anyone would know. Then again, vampires are always funny critters when it comes to paying attention to the modern world. More than any eternal creature, they live in the past. I suppose because they do not grow, really, past the point where they are turned.

He reveals a little more about his life, but not much. All I can sense is that he's hiding something, but I don't feel like it's malicious. Just a great wealth of pain.

My alarm drags me away rather suddenly.

☾O☽

I feel sad when I wake. Reaching out, I turn off the alarm and sit up, dropping my legs over the edge of the bed. With my elbows on my knees, I run my palms over my face with a long, deep breath. If I'm not careful, I won't be able to focus on anything at all today. That's not a very good thing for a cop, is it?

The first thing I do is take a shower, and I stand an extra-long time under the running water. It soothes me. It clears my mind and tempers my soul. Dalora is the fae realm of the seas, and water is the element of all my Daloran kin. New London is right on Connecticut's coast. It isn't the ocean but Long Island Sound, but still, it's water, and the smell of the sea greets me some days. The Coast Guard Academy is even here in town.

It's one of the reasons I like it.

Finally, I have to force myself out. I get dressed and eat breakfast, then head to work. I am there before Jackson tonight and find a pair of pink slips of paper, phone messages taken during the day, on my desk.

What are you? (Did not leave name.)

What are you? (Did not leave name.)

I frown, wondering if this is personal or just another LOHAV character. Those bastards. The preternatural races had barely stepped foot into the spotlight when the bigots were arising and organized. The League of Humans Against Vampires was happy to be comprehensive in their anti-preternatural stance, of course, and would hate me just as much as a vampire…

As Adrien.

I crumble both slips and toss them into my trashcan. They make a colorful addition to the other trash in the basket.

There is also PAAS: People's Army Against the Supernatural. Ironically, despite the word 'army' in their name, they are the less violent of the two. LOHAV has managed to earn the badge 'hate group' quite strongly, while PAAS spends more time skirting the line. If I have some crazy who saw my interview coming after me, chances are it's a LOHAV freak trying to rile me up.

I am apparently off in my own world because the sight of a hand with a coffee cup cutting through my line of sight startles me. Looking up, I see Jackson's curious smile. "Are you okay?"

"Of course." I laugh softly, taking the cup.

"You just seem… I don't know, kind of distant the past couple days. When I walked in just now, you were staring off into space like you were trying to see the image in one of those weird 3D pictures." At my raised brow, he waves his hand. "A fad from a while back, apparently before your time."

I shrug. "I'm fine, just a little space cadet, I guess."

He eyes me a moment longer and then nods. "As you like," he says as he pushes off from my desk and returns to his own. "Simon Allen's lawyer has finally agreed to let him speak with us, so we've got that interview set later tonight after our midnight lunch."

In reply, I nod and let that pull my focus. There is a file to go over and notes to collect, so I fill my time with that. With no more weird phone calls, just a partner with a weird sense of humor who likes to chime in every now and then, I manage to concentrate on work until 'lunch,' which is the mid-shift meal that happens in the heart of the night.

"I'm going out for lunch," I say, pushing back from my desk. "Want anything?"

"No, thanks. I brought in leftovers."

I grin at him, bumping his chair with my hip as I walk past. "So domestic."

He throws a crumpled paper ball at me. "Shut up." The grin is impossible to miss.

There is a deli just down the street from our office that is one of the happiest around because we all go there for every meal we don't eat from home, and preternatural types can have remarkable appetites. It helps that they make just damn good food, including a New England clam chowder and a lobster bisque made from local (regional, at least) seafood. They also do a blood pudding that the vampires just adore. It's made from animal blood, but the vamps will swear it's as good as the human variety. No one asks too many questions, but it's high praise.

This place is owned by what I call very smart business minds.

Since it's so close, I walk. I like to take in the air, and it is really a short trek. The street is well lit but even with all the lamps, you can't escape the feeling of the dark. It's not a bad feeling, and it's one that I've come to really like.

Something is different tonight, though. After walking for just a few minutes, I feel that 'creepy' feeling on the back of my neck. My step slows, and I try to examine the feeling, try to dissect what it is and what might be causing it. I look around, but I don't see anything out of the ordinary. I'm not the only other person out, but at first glance, I don't see anyone who is paying me any attention.

Frowning, I keep walking. I can't shake the feeling and speed up. I twitch muscles, assuring myself of my sidearm. It's not the only trick up my sleeve, but it's good to be extra aware of all the weapons in my arsenal.

But for all the adrenaline spiking in my veins, I walk into the deli without any trouble and as I glance back through the window front, I don't see anything. Am I just unsettled because of the dreams? Maybe just a little over-aware? Hypervigilant?

I try to shake the feeling as I place an order. I get it to go and return to the office. The feeling is still there as I walk back, but it seems less somehow. It's hard to describe, but since nothing happened on the walk to and from, I just have to chalk it up to me feeling weird. After all, working in law enforcement leaves one feeling paranoid a lot of time. The things you see, the things you hear, the things you have to know about... Your psyche pays a heavy price for the job, and I know that.

Still, it didn't feel like that, but since I don't have any proof to what caused the feeling, I try to just file it away and go about my job.

We do have work to do.

☾○☽

We are back on the shores of the Sea of Forever. I look out over those waters and can't stop a smile, though I don't try to.

"I wish I could understand how this is working," I say. I don't turn to see if he's there, I just know that he is. I can't tear my eyes away from the water right now, because it's just too beautiful and it calms me.

"I haven't the slightest idea, and I have been wondering," he replies.

I smile again, because I knew he was there and I was right.

"I wish I could see this, for real," he comments.

That dims my smile, and I finally look away. I turn toward him. "I wish I could see it again," I say ruefully. The wind blows in over the water, bringing the salt scent of every ocean but also the unique, sweet, almost floral scent that is a fae ocean.

He tilts his head and looks at me curiously. "Why can't you?"

Staring at him, I can't bring myself to answer at first. I haven't really ever told anyone about why I was exiled. I don't realize I'm biting my lip until it starts to hurt. Dalora is painful to think of, which is why I have generally hated dreaming about it. Somehow, it was easier to be here tonight, until I started thinking too much. I inhale deeply and smile sadly.

"I killed someone." The answer is plain. I don't try to shade it.

"What happened?" he asks.

Turning away from him, I wrap my arms around my

torso and start walking along the shore. I don't have to look to feel him walking beside me. "Violent crime is almost unheard of in many fae realms, for a variety of reasons, but it's true. However, it is not impossible. Simply put, I was attacked. I never imagined it could happen to me, but it did. In the process of fighting back, I killed him."

I could almost feel his frown. "That's self-defense," he said. "That's not your fault."

This argument could be made a thousand times, but it would never change a thing. "It doesn't matter. The idea was that I killed him instead of incapacitating him and leaving him to fae law. I was deemed violent myself and exiled."

"That's not fair," he says.

"Few things are," I reply easily as I look up at him. His brow is furrowed with his own frustration at the perceived injustice. I have seen the expression on many a face, about my story or someone else's. The silence draws on, and I wonder if either of us will speak again before I have to wake up.

"I was an artist," he says suddenly. "My sire turned me because I was beautiful. I knew it too. I was vain. Same old story. She knew that revolution was stirring and I was starving on the streets anyway, starving artist and all, and so she turned me to save me. I was grateful then, didn't really see that I was little more than a pet to her. A pretty bird kept in a cage.

"There have always been hunters," he continues. I don't say anything because I don't dare interrupt him. I want to know about him, and he's about to tell me. I just pray that my alarm doesn't go off before he finishes his story. "We were found by a skilled pair. I still don't fully know what they used on me, but I know there was silver in it. They threw it in my face, intending, I think, to burn into my brain? I don't know. It did burn. It hurt more than anything I could ever imagine."

I can't help but wince at the thought. Silver is an 'allergy' shared by almost every preternatural species, no one knows why, but some have it worse than others. The vampires get hit hard, and I can't imagine getting it in my eyes. It must have felt like acid.

"We got out without getting staked or burnt or beheaded," he is saying. "She got me out, but nothing could be done. The silver had burned my eyes bad enough to blind me and to scar me, badly."

I'm shocked and swallow hard. "That's why you were so upset when I asked about you being an artist." The pieces fall into place.

It's his turn to smile ruefully at me. "Yes," he says. "I can't paint anymore, because of the blindness. The only things I can see are what I see in my dreams and in my memories." He pauses and looks out over the sea. "She abandoned me, because of the scarring. I wasn't...pretty anymore, and that's not what she wanted. So she left."

"That's terrible!" The words are out of my mouth before my brain has even realized it thought them, though I don't regret saying it. "And you're...still in France?"

"Yes," he said. "I wandered a while, but it was hard and I hurt. My eyes hurt, and my spirit hurt. Eventually, I went to ground. I've been there since. It's not much of a life, but I have these vivid dreams." He meets my eyes again. He opens his mouth, but all that comes out is an obnoxious, loud beeping.

☾O☽

"Damn," I exclaim when I realize my alarm has gone off.

There is a pain in my heart as I get out of bed. Perhaps that is why we have connected so well, because we share the loss and betrayal. My homeland turned on me and his sire turned on him for things that weren't our fault and that we couldn't change. But I forged ahead and made a life for myself, while he...clearly didn't, although I don't know enough about vampire lore to know what going to ground actually means. In my line of work, it usually means going into hiding. Something tells me that it means more in his case.

I want to find out, and if you want to know about vampires, it is best to go to the source, and lucky me, I happen to know a pair.

It's still light out when I get up, so too early. I go through my usual morning routine, but I can't get him out of my head. It's like he's invaded my waking world as surely as he has invaded my dreaming one, yet I can't seem to mind that much.

At the office, I get that weird feeling again as I walk into the building. I stop at the door and look around, but nothing. I curse myself for being so rattled and go to my desk, where I gratefully find that there aren't any messages waiting for me. I log onto my computer and go through my work email.

The day comes and goes. Just another day at the FBI. Jackson leaves and goes to find his girlfriend, while I leave and head into Adelheid. It's not a terribly long drive, and the highway is a busier place than it used to be, what with all the preternatural folk going about their business.

Once in town, I go to the Stanton Agency. Walking in the front door, Madison St John—the werewolf secretary— smiles politely but then blinks at me in surprise. "Agent Kai," she greets curiously. "What are… Is there a problem?"

"No," I say quickly, smiling to try to put her at ease. "I was just wondering if your boss was in. It's not official business."

"Sure…" Madison nods slowly then gets up to go knock on the door behind her. She pokes her head in and has a conversation I can't hear. After a moment, she steps back and waves me to go in.

"Agent Kai," Sadie greets.

Sadie Stanton, vampire, owner of the Stanton Agency, poster girl for preternatural rights, and well-known Adelheid citizen. She's smiling just as curiously as her secretary had.

"Ms. Stanton," I greet. "Or do you go by Mrs. Johnston now?"

She grins. Her fangs are 'at rest,' but you can still see their points. "Legally, I'm still Stanton, but I get plenty of mail with Johnston on it so call me whatever you like, though Sadie is just fine." She waves at a chair in front of her desk, and I take a seat.

"You can call me Posey. I'm not here on business." I pause, trying to think of how best to frame this and wondering if I'm about to ask some sort of top-secret vampire things. "I wanted to talk to you about...vampires." Her brows rise. "Specific things, really. Thing." I wince, knowing that I'm sounding way too stupid to be a representative of the FBI. "I'm sorry, let me start again. I am just not sure how best to ask this."

"Straightforward is usually best," she says smoothly.

"Yes." I smile. "I have a new friend, who is a vampire. He made a comment the other night that I don't fully understand. I haven't been able to ask him, and I'm not sure I will." How do you explain that the man of your dreams is not a euphemism? "So I wanted to see if I could ask you."

Curiosity is very clear in her eyes, but she nods. "Ask and if I can, I'll answer."

I pause and reconsider, but then I charge ahead. "What does 'going to ground' mean?"

It's now equally obvious that this was not the question she expected. "Vampires are not true immortals, but we come close. The most amusing description I've heard is that we're like Newton's Law of Motion. We keep going unless something very specific stops us. One thing that doesn't stop us like it would a human is, literally, going into the ground. We don't starve the way humans do. It can take centuries. If I vampire decides to do so, usually for some emotional reason, they can bury themselves in the earth and just...exist there."

That was much more depressing than I had thought. "Why would one of your kind do that?"

She shrugs slightly. "There can be a variety of reasons," she says. "It's usually some kind of trauma, or the vampire version of severe depression."

"Are they...awake during the nights?"

"Yes," she says plainly. I appreciate her honesty, but there is a certain amount of horror in the idea of living that way. It would be like waking up in your own coffin, rather literally, every single night. Although I know he must be able to come out if he wants to, it's still almost painful to think of the fact that he had chosen to live that way. But then, he clearly lives his life in his dreams rather than the real world...

Finally, I realize that I've been sitting there without saying anything and laugh sheepishly. "It sounds like a really...tough way to live."

She smiles faintly. "It's not living," she says. "It's existing, which I guess is how it really is like a vampire depression. It's possible to come back from, if the vampire wants." She echoes my thoughts of just a few moments ago. There is another short silence before she says, "Why do you ask?"

She has the right to ask, considering what I just asked her. Still, I don't know that I am able to properly tell someone about it. "I don't know that I know how to explain," I say honestly, "but it's something I needed to know."

☾O☽

I drive back to New London and to my apartment. It's a ground floor one, accessible from the road without a lobby or guarded door. More like a rented house, although it's not really a house. I park on the street and go in, still thinking over the conversation with Sadie. She had been very kind to answer my haphazard questions. Really, for someone who interrogated people as part of her livelihood, I couldn't stop thinking about how I'd flubbed that chat.

Tonight, I don't even bother to take my usual shower. I take off my shoes and change into a long T-shirt, slipping into bed and settling back. My desire to be asleep is strong enough to pull me straight into slumber.

It's the sea, again. This time, though, it's the coast of Connecticut. I didn't go to my old home but to my current one. I have to wonder what that means, if anything at all.

"This is beautiful too," he says beside me, and I turn to him. I smile, although something breaks in my heart when I see him now. I wonder where he is, buried somewhere in the French countryside. I wonder what he looks like. I know now that this is the vision of his past. I get it, but there's something distant about it.

"Is something wrong?" he asks me.

I shake my head. "Not at all." My mind does drift briefly back to the phone calls and the sense of being followed, but I dismiss it quickly. It doesn't matter here. "I can't seem to stop thinking about you." It seems safe to admit it here, like everything else.

He flashes that smile. "My thoughts are much filled as well." Suddenly, I see the same sorrow flash through his eyes as I felt in myself just moments ago. It's only a dream, after all.

Taking a step toward him, he watches me as I draw close. I smile to reassure him, but then I hear a noise. It sounds like... I'm not sure, but it's not supposed to be here. My body tenses, and I jerk my head to one side. Footsteps. I hear footsteps, like shoes on hardwood, but there's no flooring here.

He sees the look on my face and his is immediately filled with concern. "Posey, what's going on?" he asks urgently. His hands grip my arms, and I wish I could think about how it feels, but I can't afford to.

"Something is wrong," I say. "There is someone in my h—"

☾○☽

Abruptly, I wake to the sound of someone coming through my bedroom door. They knock over a small table next to the frame, and the crash echoes through the room. I sit straight up in bed to see the figure of a man in the dim light. I can't make out his face very well, but I'm sure I don't know him.

I should be scared, but I'm just pissed.

In my haste to get to bed, I dropped my holster with my jacket and it's on the floor. I don't know who is faster. He knows I'm awake now, and there's that long, frozen moment… before he lunges for me. I jump back on the bed and out of his grasp. I grab the lamp on the bedside table and swing, hard and fast. Its arc picks up speed and it collides with the side of his head. He grunts unintelligibly and staggers back. I'm already driving forward, swinging the lamp—which is a metal L-shape with a metal shade—a second time, catching him on the other side of the head.

That one puts him on the ground. I jump off the bed and land next to him, wrenching his unconscious hands behind his back and tying them with the lamp cord that was ripped out of the wall so unceremoniously that the wires are showing where the plug once existed. I secure the knots and just as I check them, I hear a soft 'whoosh' sound.

I whirl around, readying myself for another attack, but instead I see…

"Adrien!"

"I was so afraid of what was happening," he said. "I'm… Well, I can port when I have to and just followed my dream-sense to you."

A million questions float through my mind, like what dream-sense is, but I don't ask them. Now isn't the time, and I'm too distracted by him.

In life, he's a lot thinner than his dream form, but if he's been starving himself... His hair is still long and tied back. He's still tall...but his eyes. His eyes are a pale silver color, both of them and completely, and there are scars around them. They are like flower blossoms, where the eyes are the center and the scars bloom outwards.

"God, you're beautiful," I hear myself breathing the words.

"Are you okay?" he asks, still sounding scared and like he didn't hear what I said.

Then I realize that he can't see the situation, and I gasp softly. "Yes," I say, looking at the man on the floor. "I took care of things. But I have to call Jackson." Scrambling for my cell phone in my jacket pocket, I grab it and my gun (just to be safe) and call my partner. I sit Adrien on my bed to wait, and Jackson comes with a couple local uniforms. Adrien raises some questions, but I put them off and give my statement. They cart the man off and ask if I need to see a doctor, but I assure him I'm fine. I'll learn more tomorrow.

It seems like forever before they're gone.

When they are, I sit beside Adrien on the bed. He has been silent through this whole thing, but I can't blame him.

"I was so scared when you looked that way and vanished suddenly," he says softly. "I haven't teleported much. I'm not usually that good at it, even though it was a skill I had after being turned. Vampire skills can vary in strength, and I wasn't strong...until tonight. I think my fear improved it." He smiles ruefully, his face tilting toward me.

"I'm a cop," I say with a little mirth. "I can take care of myself, but I appreciate that you came for me."

He laughs softly. "Well, now I feel a little silly. And now… Well, you've seen me."

I wrap my hand around his. It's surprisingly strong as I squeeze it and he squeezes back. "I have seen you," I say. "You're beautiful."

His expression quickly shifts to incredulousness. "Don't tease me…"

"I'm serious," I say. "Even…" I lift my other hand to trace the edges of the scars. "Even these are beautiful."

"You're just trying to be kind."

My brow knits. I don't know how to convince him of what I mean, then an idea comes to me. I look across my room to the violin on its stand. Another gift of the fae, but at least this one I was able to bring with me: my music magic. I can work by singing, but the violin is my preferred instrument. "What if I can show you?"

He looks taken back. "How… How?"

"Wait and…*see*," I say. I squeeze his hand again and then get up, crossing the room to take up my instrument. I haven't made time to play in a week or so, but it's one of those things that I never forget. I place it on my chin, feeling the gentle hum of its enchantment, and then place the bow on the strings. I form in my mind the magic I want to weave: to evoke a waking dream for him, as seen through my eyes and as I feel it. Then, I begin to play. I keep the tune soft and slow, pulling magic from myself, my instrument, from him, from the land all around us, for the land has its own magic.

I play. He looks uncertain, almost frightened, at first. But then he grows still, and I can feel that the spell has settled to him. His look of surprise tells me that it's working, and I smile as I keep my eyes on him and show him what I see and what I feel when I see him. He smiles, and it is as brilliant as the sun and as pleasing as the sea.

For the first time ever, I'm happy that I dream.

GUTTED

Content Warning: This story contains references to child exploitation and extreme violence that may be uncomfortable for some readers.

My small hands were not naturally of a good size to shuffle a deck of cards larger than the ones you play poker with, but they had developed a dexterity over the centuries that allowed me to do it now without trouble. I ruffled the Tarot deck nine times and then set it on the floor before me, cutting it into three piles with my left hand.

Reassembling the deck, I drew and then laid down three cards. I flipped them over and examined each one in turn. By the time I was flipping over the final, I didn't have time to look closely when I heard a knock upstairs. I looked up at the ceiling, briefly wondering who was here. I wasn't curious enough to go look, but I wondered. Then I heard the footsteps moving over my head, the door at the top of the stairs opened, and I knew someone was coming down for me.

Someone knocked on my door. "Abby?" It was Shayna Harel, lead warden of the Coven House. Even after a decade or so of living in the United States, she still had her Israeli accent and a problem with English idioms, kind of like that character on television.

I didn't answer, but I watched the door because I knew she wouldn't stop there.

She knocked again and then opened it, peering in. Her head surveyed the room with the experience of someone in security or the police. Rumor had it she was former Israeli Mossad, but she'd never admitted as much to me. When her eyes fell on me and found that I was already watching her, she twitched a little.

"I never like it when you do that, Abby," she said plainly. I liked her for her plainspoken nature.

"Too bad," I said with a shrug, which wasn't the most impressive of gestures from the physical body of a ten-year-old girl. "What do you want?"

"There are people here to talk to you," she said, opening the door the rest of the way and letting the wooden frame of my basement lair box in her strongly shaped body. If it weren't for the whole ancient vampire thing I had going on, I was pretty sure she could break me physically in half like a bit of twig.

That was strange, I thought. No one ever came here to see me, who didn't already live here at least and even those visits were few. Even among the vampires, I was considered 'creepy,' and take a moment to let that sink in: even the vampires thought I was creepy.

She seemed to read the debate in my eyes. "These are the kind of people who will come down here to remove you," she clarified. "In handcuffs, if need be."

"Cops?" That was even more of a surprise. I couldn't think of anything I'd done recently to earn a trip to the police station. I took a few moments to wrack my brain, but I still couldn't think of anything. I barely left the Coven House, so how could I?

"I suppose I don't have much choice then, do I?" I sneered.

Glancing down, I saw the final card that I had flipped over in the 'future' position.

Judgment.

☾○☽

Reaching the 'receiving room,' as it was called here at the edict of our rather proper leader, I was greeted by several faces. None of them I really wanted to see, truth be told. I recognized Jade, of course, as coven leader. Sitting in the largest armchair with the presence of the vampire, even her diminutive stature commanded the room. It also helped that our visitors were all seated on one sofa together, looking like a small group of children.

I recognized the first two: Detective Sam Moore and Special Agent Jackson Lang. The first was part of the Adelheid Police Department, while the latter was part of the preternatural branch of the New London satellite office of the FBI. These weren't exactly people I met on a regular basis, but it's a small town and a close-knit community, even for those of us who weren't necessarily eager to be part of it.

The one of the end, though, I didn't recognize.

All but Jade stood up when I walked in. "Albine?" the stranger asked. Immediately, I picked up on the British accent, and that made this interesting, at least for the moment. The fact that he used my 'real' name was another shocker. Although it was not the world's greatest kept secret, it wasn't commonly used either.

"I am," I said, folding my arms over my flat chest. I didn't make an imposing figure, I knew. Still, I could tear out a throat pretty easily if I needed to. "What do the police need me for?"

"We are here to question you," the Brit was still the one talking, "about Jack the Ripper."

I didn't say anything, but every muscle in my very slim body tensed. Not for the reasons they would think, I was sure, but tense all the same. They asked me to come to the station, and I agreed with a nod. They drove me. They assured me that I wasn't under arrest, but they did want to talk to me. I tried to figure out how the hell this came about.

Now I was sitting in the interrogation room. The chair was uncomfortable and too big for me. I was used to that. The Brit was looking down at me. Sam and Jackson were in the room because this was their 'turf,' but it was obviously the Brit's game.

"I'm Chief Detective Inspector Morton," he introduced himself at last. "You are not under arrest and are here of your own free will."

"You said that part already," I said flatly. "Yes, I came voluntarily. Even so, it wasn't like I really felt like I had a choice. A cop flies across the ocean to talk to you about news that should've been dead over a century before and you don't turn him down. So ask your questions and let's get this over with."

Morton glanced back at the natives, but Sam smirked and shrugged. Yes, I was like this all the time. He looked a bit flustered, which was surprising for a cop, but maybe he wasn't used to dealing with miniature vampiric dolls with bad attitudes. He regained his composure quickly and continued. "I suppose some explanation is in order, Ms. Albine."

I tilted my head. "Just Albine."

He blinked. He was tall, clean, and well put together. With blonde hair neatly combed and blue eyes, he reminded me a little of a Ken doll, though presumably with all of his properly human body parts.

"Albine," he corrected himself. "I'm sure you're curious as to why you're here."

"You could say that." I considered making one of my usual suicide quips but decided against it. In a room with three cops, it seemed inappropriate. Contrary to what my fellow Coven House members might think, I do know what's appropriate. I just usually don't care.

"As I'm sure you're aware, preternatural legalization came to Britain in this past year," he went on. I stared at him as he spoke. He looked like he wasn't certain what to think about that fact, but I chose not to press it. I did want to know what prompted this visit. This was something that I never wanted to go back to. "As such, there have been...new avenues to things that were heretofore impossible."

I blinked once. "How many more connecting flights are we going to take until we get to the point, Chief Detective Inspector?"

His pale brows knit slightly. "I'm getting there. One of those things is animators, or in this case, a necromancer. One of your acquaintance, Sarah Beaumont, was hired to raise one of the victims of Jack the Ripper. Legal permission was obtained for an exhumation of Marie Jeanette Kelly."

If my blood hadn't already been cold, it would have gone cold then. *No, not Mary...*

My face must have changed, despite my best efforts. I could see it reflected in a change in his expression. "Yes. I, frankly, did not believe it possible to raise someone who had been dead for more than a hundred years, with no intact body to speak of, but apparently the magic of a strong necromancer is stronger than even I could presume. The magic enabled speech."

I knew how it worked, but I didn't tell him. "Was it... successful?" I asked softly.

"Yes," he said solemnly. "Somewhat."

"Somewhat?"

He nodded slowly. "She...screamed. Nonstop and almost entirely incoherently." His pale eyes somehow seemed to get paler, with that haunted look I had seen in many faces. I had seen that same look, even worse, in the faces of the cops who had seen Mary Kelly's body when it had been newly slain. Those men would never be the same.

I could almost hear her screaming in my mind when he said it, and I had to close my eyes, even though I had long since grown unable to cry. (Vampires have nothing in their tear ducts, after all.) I wished I could, though. Again, I wished I could weep for poor Mary.

When I opened my eyes again, Morton was staring at me. "Her screams were almost entirely incoherent, but there was one word that came out clear. She screamed a name."

"Albine," I said for him.

"Albine," he confirmed, nodding slowly.

Since I knew Sarah Beaumont, she would have recognized my name and have been able to tell them that yes, in fact, maybe I was there.

"So, what can you tell me about Jack the Ripper?" he asked.

"I can tell you that there was no Jack the Ripper," I replied plainly.

The room was silent for a long time. I didn't do anything to break that as they all stared at me and I took turns with which one I stared back at, although it was primarily Morton since he was sitting across from me. He looked like he didn't know what to say, and I was hardly surprised by that.

"What are you talking about?" This was from Sam, who now pulled up a chair because the conversation was impossible to resist. "Everyone knows that there was a Jack the Ripper."

"No," I corrected without hesitation. "Everyone *thinks* there was, but we all know that just because a lot of people believe something, it doesn't mean that it's true."

"But there was evidence..." Morton stammered slightly. This was not going how he had expected.

I snorted. It was as close to a laugh as I ever got, especially when this was no laughing matter. "What evidence?"

"M.O.," Sam said.

"There was no real pattern," I said. "Throats were slashed. That is hardly a distinguishable method of killing. Only three of the victims had organs removed, and only two had them removed in similar means. Two does not truly make the pattern of a serial killer. And even back in the day, they were arguing about whether the killer showed medical skill; some of the deaths did and some didn't. Know why? They weren't the same people."

"Location," Morton said. "They all took place within a comparatively contained area."

I shook my head. "Do you know how many people lived in that cramped area? There is more violence statistically in crowded urban environments, people don't like being sardines, but it doesn't mean that it's all the same person."

Now Jackson sat down. "The letters to the press that linked them and gave them the name."

Morton looked at him. "Most people don't believe those letters were written by the killer nowadays as it is," he said so I didn't have to. "I personally believe that someone in the press did it to stir up circulation."

"Was there ever a time when the press wasn't full of vampires without fangs?" Sam sighed.

"No," I replied easily. "Any witness sightings around the times of the murders gave accounts of differing people, and because none of them could agree, most of them were dismissed as not the killer. There was even the Thames torso murder, a woman's body without a womb, but it was dismissed as not Ripper..."

"But?" Sam prompted.

"They decided there was a single killer for the others, so they started fitting evidence to their theories instead of theories to the evidence," I replied. "They could have made arrests, but culprits and suspects were cast aside for one murder because they had an alibi or were incapable of having committed one of the others."

Morton shook his head like he was in a fog. "How do you know these things?"

My mind was already rolling down the stony staircases of my history and through worn doors on rusty hinges that I had wanted to keep shut tight for the rest of my days, which I knew could be a great many—despite my best efforts—but I still wanted to keep it shut. Now I was tumbling down and through the door, breaking things open that I didn't want to.

"I was there," I said. "I was living in Whitechapel in the eighteen-eighties." I paused. "I was a prostitute, and I knew these women."

I had been waiting for the look that I knew would come when I revealed that bit of news, and it took no time at all. It was equal parts horror, disgust, and fascination. I gave them a little time to process it.

"You..." Sam started and stopped. "But look at you."

"Get it out of your system now," I sneered. "It was a different time, and that didn't matter so much. I fed certain needs, earned the coin to keep a nice dark place for my daytime hours, and that was what mattered."

People might wonder why I didn't just let myself be roasted, given my predilection for ending my un-life, but it wasn't so much a thing of mine then. I didn't like being a vampire in the body of a little kid then any more than now, but I was...different. Everything was different.

"A small vampire in a place like the abyss can see much and be seen little," I said.

"So what did you see?" Morton asked, like he couldn't believe that he was having this conversation. I couldn't blame him. When could some CDI from London have guessed he'd be talking with a two-thousand-year-old child about the 'greatest serial killer mystery' of all time?

I looked at my frail little hands and twisted a silver-colored ring where it sat around my middle finger. "It started with Martha Tabram," I began.

"Tabram," Morton interrupted. "She wasn't one of the canonical five."

I really did try to restrain my *are you an idiot* look, but I think I failed. "If there was no Jack the Ripper, then why does the canonical five matter?"

He nodded. "Fair enough."

"There were eleven murders around that time, those few months, termed as the Whitechapel Murders, and the five assigned to Jack were part of them. For me, it started with Martha, because she was my friend."

I felt surrounded by the stench and the smoke of the abyss once again, with the noise and the crush of humanity. "It was so stupid," I said with a laugh that sounded tearful, even if there weren't real tears within it. "She was working, went off with a soldier, and got killed by the jealous wife.

"Some thought she was Ripper, before he settled his pattern, because all the stab wounds were to her abdomen and throat. That's not M.O. but logistics. You have someone before you who is roughly the same size and you go to kill them, you hit throat and stomach." I waved my hands at all the idiots of the past. "But...something did feel different in Whitechapel then, with her death. I didn't know what it was, really, but it felt wrong. I got worried. And I started keeping my eyes open for my other friends.

"And then..." I sighed, clasping my hands and pressing my forehead to them. "Then Mary Ann Nichols died, and the madness soon followed.

"Mary was the first who was 'ripped,' and the viciousness of that is what started the real furor over the Whitechapel Murders. The papers were already on it even before the second murder in what is called the canonical five," I continued.

I stopped twisting the ring on my finger, battered thing that it was, and pulled it off. I set it on the table between us. "When I'm done," I said, feeling flat and defeated about the trip I was taking, "pick this up."

Morton began to reach for it, but I stopped him. "Not you," I said and let my gaze slide to Sam. "Her."

A striking woman, her gray-green eyes were curious for a moment before the light of understanding shone in them. She turned to Morton. "I'm a psychometric and should be able to gain impressions and some history off that item."

He nodded slowly, although I got the impression that he didn't really get it.

"So who killed Mary Ann Nichols?" Morton asked. It was still painfully clear that he felt very out of his depth, and I didn't intend to work at making him feel better. Not that I planned to make him feel worse, but I'm not the best in the world at offering comfort.

"Understand that I don't know names," I said. "I happened to be near Buck's Row. I heard the scream and rushed to the sound. There was a man just rushing off. Maybe he heard me, though I can't imagine how. The leather apron that everyone talked so much about." I rubbed my eyes. "I got to her. She gurgled. 'The butcher,' she croaked just before dying. I wanted to stay, but the witness—Charles Cross—came up. They think he's the one who scared off the man, and maybe he was, but he scared me off. I didn't know her well. There would be cops... I couldn't tangle with cops, not being what I am."

They stared at me, and I feared they could see through me to the things I felt. I knew the look. They were cops, and a potential witness had fled the scene. They didn't think much of me for that.

They would think even less of me by the time I was done.

"The butcher was one of her clients," I explained. "He was always violent, and he never wanted to pay. Drank plenty. Then again, most everyone did. I got drunk just off feeding…"

Morton paled a little.

"What about Annie Chapman?"

"They suspected her killer had medical training. She had her throat cut and organs removed. A doctor. Whispers were that it was some foreigner who couldn't practice in London and took it out on her. I don't know for sure, but it makes sense."

I continued before they had to ask. "Elizabeth Stride was killed by a man who didn't want to pay. Most didn't and a lot of them got away without doing so. Long Liz could make a point when she had to. I tried to stop him, but…it was too late. I could have torn him apart, but I didn't." I paused and thought. "There are people now who don't think Stride was Ripper interrupted but just happened to have her throat slashed during that time.

"Eddowes was pregnant and had sought the help of an abortionist. It was…a hellish thing back in those days, or could be, and this particular woman seemed to be going around the bend. Even other girls were noticing how weird she was getting. Angry. Violent. She took it out on the girls, and most wouldn't consider even talking to her. Catherine did, got turned away…but apparently the woman was just too mad by then.

"Catherine was seen with a sailor around one-thirty. Just minutes later, they were attacked by the abortionist. A woman named Sophie Maddox. He took off and Maddox worked fast, carved the hell out of Catherine."

"And how do you know *this*?" Morton asked. He was getting dubious, I could tell.

"I found the sailor while everyone was with Catherine's body. I made him talk, and I bit him. I was angry at his cowardice. I didn't kill him. He somehow got away and vanished for good, and so did Maddox."

"And you still didn't talk to anyone about any of this?" Jackson asked.

I met his eyes reluctantly. "No," I said. "I couldn't... I couldn't risk being exposed. I was a tiny vampire living in eighteen-eighties London. I..."

"What about the writing on the wall?" Morton said.

"Maybe Maddox pushing attention off herself, or someone just caught up in the fervor. I don't know."

There was a long strain of silence now.

We all knew what was next, but I wasn't volunteering this time. My cold, dead heart wanted to crawl up my throat.

It was Morton who asked. "Alright," he said slowly. The wheels in his head were audibly turning as he tried to process everything I had said. The idea of 'Jack the Ripper' had been so long entrenched that it was hard to change it. I was flying in the face of more than a hundred years, but I was one of the few who could. "What about Marie Jeanette Kelly?"

"Poor Mary," I whispered, staring at the ring again. "Mary Kelly...was my fault."

☾○☽

8th November 1888

It never ceased to amaze me how fast things can go.

The night was a cold and wet one, but the 'unfortunates' were still out. We were looked down upon by almost all of society, including those who frequented us, but I was certain that we were the hardest working people in the city. What else was there for the poor to do, anyways, but drink and fuck? The former and latter feeding into one another in a never-ending, vicious cycle that kept down those who were down.

Not much by way of clientele were out, however, in the chilly wetness. I ducked my tiny frame under the overhang of an inn and was startled a moment later when another woman ducked under it beside me. Like every human adult, she was larger than I was, but distinguishable past that by her long, red hair.

"Oi, wet one out tonight," she said with her heavy, 'low-class' English accent. It was a linguistic affection that I lacked but explained by my being foreign born and orphaned here when my parents died. The first, true. The latter, less so. My parents had never set foot in England, and they never would. By 1888, they had been dead and in the ground for over seventeen centuries.

"It is," I agreed. Her rough clothing made it clear that she and I were members of the same profession, and I took no issue with any one of us. Had she been else-wise, I'd have been less concerned with being friendly. "Not much coin to be made either, apparently."

She eyed me up and down, perhaps calculating my age. I stood out because of that, although it wasn't entirely unheard of. Well, the real me was, but the image I projected was not.

"I guess all the cocks are scared off by a bit of cold weather," she quipped after a moment, smirking. "Afraid it'll shrivel up and be no use to them."

That made me laugh. "I'd think you'd be right about that." I offered her my small hand. "Albine." I don't know why I gave her my real name, I never told it to anyone, but for some reason, I wanted her to know. "But everyone calls me Abby." I didn't give her a last name, because I didn't have one.

"Mary," she said. "Mary Kelly."

Little could I know at that time what her name would come to mean to me for the next century and beyond. If I could have known, I would have walked away and never set eyes upon her again. Some would say that it wouldn't have mattered, because what was meant to be would always be meant to be. I don't know that I believe that now or believed it then, but the guiding hand that keeps me from the fate I try to gain for myself does make me suspicious.

"I have a little money from tonight," she said, "if you want to get something to eat."

"I'm not hungry," I told her. It was the truth, but I of course did not tell her all of it, which was that I couldn't eat what she did. It struck me, however, the idea that she couldn't possibly have much and was offering to share it with me. Kindness always has been a commodity in sparse supply, I've found, and I was touched by hers. In turn, it prompted me to feel some of my own. "I have a room tonight, if you need."

Of course, the moment I said it, I wanted to kick myself. How would I explain the state I'd fall into as soon as dawn hit? Fortunately for me, she told me she already had a room at Miller's Court and thus did not need my charity any more than I needed hers, but I could tell she was as touched by it as I.

She invited me back to this room, which had so recently been vacated by her domestic partner, and we shared some liquor. Drinking is acceptable to the vampire body, while food is not. I thought about the other women I'd known these past few months that I knew no longer, taken at the hands of the papers' darling Jack. I knew the truth, of course, but it didn't matter, because dead was dead. Well, real dead was different than me dead, but they were not walking among us lacking a heartbeat. They were cold and in the ground, and I missed those who had been my friends. I had few.

Mary was sweet, however, and shared the bottle with me. She drank more than I and talked far more too. After

I had heard about her childhood and how she'd ended up here, as well as the man with who she'd been living and how she ended up so unfortunate, she fell asleep with the bottle still in her hand.

Dawn was coming, but I took the time to put a blanket over her and set the bottle away before slipping into the darkness before the dawn. I made it to my own room, shabby and tiny as it was, just before the sun rose high enough to drive me down into the coma that encases all such beings as I.

☾O☽

There was something happening in Whitechapel at that time, and more than just the murders and the Ripper furor, although admittedly—in retrospect—I realize that it may have had something to do with those things.

For some months, I had felt something...off. The rise of violence, or the excess to the violence itself, seemed to feed off that something. After a month or so, I began to suspect what it was. Autumn was descending, winter would come soon, and maybe it was that change that made me feel more, but I knew that a new preternatural being had entered London. It was similar and yet different than I.

There was a new kind of hunter in my city, and it was closing in on my little patch of territory more and more. I should have left long before, I knew, but I didn't want to. This had become my home, and I liked the people...but that night, the night of November 9th, I had decided I needed to go. The hunter was getting too close, and it was the sort not so easy to escape.

I awoke in time to see the sunset. Age has its benefits for a vampire, and I did enjoy seeing sunrises and sunsets. That night, I took my time to enjoy it because it was to be the last I'd see from that little corner of London. Not that it was as pretty from that place, but still, it was mine and I took it for what it was.

I owned little, for I needed little, but I had it packed and was on my way out, when...

"Abby!" Mary's voice startled me, and I whirled around. Every human has their own scent, and hers was already familiar. She smiled when she saw me, and I couldn't help but smile back. "The weather is clearer out tonight, isn't it?"

I looked up and then nodded. "It does seem to be that." We both still had our shawls about us, although I knew she needed hers more than I needed mine. But I didn't like to let my body get too cold. Customers could tell and it tended to bother them.

She put her arm around my shoulders and started walking me. I could tell she had already been drinking, but who could blame her. "I thought we'd take a turn on the streets together. No one should walk alone, after all."

Opening my mouth, I started to say that I was on my way out but couldn't seem to get the words said while she was walking and chatting in such a friendly way. "At least until there's business, eh?"

Mary laughed. "Aye, that. Most men don't like being watched, gives them nerves about their performance and all that." We laughed, but we knew that when men tended to get that way, it was our faces they took it out on. The ones walking the streets didn't get the "nice" ones, after all. We got the ones who tended to speak with their fists.

Or knives, like...

The sky was mostly dark, and our paths were only lit by the lanterns and a limited amount of moonlight that could pry its way through the smoggy sky. There were a fair number of people walking back and forth, many of them also drinking already, but none that turned their eyes to either of us like we were going to be collecting our rent.

We turned down another lane that wound between buildings, and there were less people and a worse feeling.

I stopped, and Mary was forced to stop with me. "What's wrong?" she asked.

"There's…" I began, but how could I explain? I opened my eyes wide and inhaled deeply through my nose, but the scent of Whitechapel did not allow much distinction. "Come, we need to go." My voice was tight with urgency, and I kept my lips close together. My fangs were already descending in my concern, and I didn't want her to see. I grabbed her by the arm and started us walking as she protested, confused, but we didn't get many steps.

A large form seemingly melted out of the shadows and grabbed me by the slender shoulder, hauling my small self away from Mary and into the shadows from where it came.

"Dhampir," I spat, instantly knowing what it was.

Dhampir. The very, very rare offspring of a vampire and a human. It takes the aligning of such stars that it truly happens perhaps once every thousand years or so, but they take on traits of both sides of their heritage and resent the vampire. It seems inborn that they do, and historically, their human mother—for the mother is always the human— would instill in them further hate of their fathers. Dhampirs almost always become hunters of vampires.

They are nearly as strong as us, and that makes them hard to fight. And he was more than twice my size, which made it even harder. He had all the advantage as he threw me up against the stone wall and hissed.

Forgetting all about where we were, I hissed back. My mouth was open, and my fangs were fully descended. With one hand free, I grabbed his slicked-back hair and ripped as hard as I could to one side. His grip loosened as I tore a handful free. I lunged forward to try to get my teeth into his neck, but his arms were too long and as soon as he felt my movement, that grip was iron-like again and stiff to hold me far away.

I screamed words that no one my apparent age should know and in many a language. My limited vampire magic slunk from me and tried to touch that part of him that was vampire, but it did not touch him enough. He shifted one large hand to my throat, not to suffocate me—because he knew that was impossible—but to hold me solidly in place while he reached for his long knife.

Before he could do much about it, however, I heard a grunt behind him and he shouted. I was dropped to the ground and when he spun around, I saw a small dagger sticking out of his back and Mary backing up against the wall, screaming bloody murder. He began to stalk toward her and I leaped, throwing my tiny body onto his back and biting his neck. I felt his sickly blood splatter back at me. Dhampir blood turned out to be more disgusting than a straight vampire's. He shouted again.

Shrill whistles echoed down the alley, and the heavy boot treads of the bobbies came toward us. The dhampir knew he shouldn't kill humans and took off. I spat his blood out and took off after him, both to pursue him and avoid the cops.

I lost him and had to press myself back into the shadows as the cops, undoubtedly sent on by Mary, rushed in the direction he had gone. I knew that they would never catch him, but let them try. It would keep him busy. I left my hiding place and hastily wiped off my face as I returned to find Mary standing with her arms around herself, trembling.

"You tried to save me," I said with a weak smile.

"Of course," she said. "We should look out for one another."

I nodded and took her arm. The cops would be done with her, or they would be now, and I guided her back to her room at Miller's Court. I settled her down on the bed and just handed her the bottle, sitting beside her.

"Who was that man?" she asked, still shaky.

"I don't know," I said. It was only partly a lie. I knew *what* he was but not *who* he was. "I guess he didn't like the look of me much."

She smiled weakly and took a sip of the cheap liquor.

I was feeling weak too and realized I needed to feed. It had been a while, and the energy expended in the fight made it more of a necessity. There felt like something else, something in the blood or psychic aura of that dhampir, that made me weak. I needed fresh blood.

"I need to go out," I said.

"What, why?" she asked with true alarm. Her pale skin seemed to get paler.

"I need to get some food," I said. It wasn't a lie. "I'll be fine, will stay to the bright lit streets, but I want you to stay here. You look ready to fall down, and I want you to rest, okay?"

She eyed me uncertainly. I knew that she didn't want to let me go out alone, but after what had happened, she didn't want to go back out. I took her hand. "Don't worry," I said and then let it go. I knew I was cold to the touch and didn't want to worry her more. "I'll be right back. Stay here."

I left in a hurry before she could argue with me.

It turned out to be another mistake on my part. I was making many of them, but this would be the final nail in the coffin, rather literally.

The time grew late, and it took longer than I wanted to find the right person. I preferred to feed on people that I didn't feel bad about, which took a certain kind of scumbag. Then I had to get them or find them alone. I was also keeping my senses out for the dhampir, but I recognized a certain... aura almost everywhere I went, and I wondered just how far his strange psychic orbit was floating through Whitechapel and how many people, and events, it had been touching.

I had no idea what time it was once I finally found the right person, cornered and caught him. I fed enough to clear the fog from my mind, then left him alive. I preferred to not kill them when possible, and who would believe their story?

Then I hurried back to Mary's room, but I had gotten further from it than I realized and it took longer than I thought it would.

I could smell the blood from a ways away. I just...knew. I knew it was her. I smelled the blood and the very distinct odor of a body being opened, which is more than blood. And I felt the same 'vibe' I had felt when being attacked by the dhampir. I broke into a run and saw the window, looking in and seeing...

She was torn apart. There were body parts in places where body parts shouldn't be, and even I, a vampire of nearly nineteen hundred years, was sickened. If I could have vomited, I would have. I was frozen in place. I wanted to go in or call someone or do something, but the door opened, and Mary's butcher walked out.

The dhampir. Revenge. She had stabbed him, protecting me...

"You bastard," I cried and launched myself at him. He took off, and I pursued. He wanted to get us somewhere before the humans came, and I didn't want to let him get that far. He could probably kill me once he turned on me, but all I saw was red...

I didn't realize just how long had passed, though. I realized that not all the red I saw was my anger, or the imprint of Mary's corpse on my eyes. It was the sun. It was rising.

Skidding to a stop, I wanted to keep after him but knew that the day's coma would force me down and then he'd kill me at his leisure. I cried out, unable to cry, and turned and ran away from that moment. I ran to somewhere dark that would not be easily found, buried myself just before the sun rose, and I knew no more.

☾ O ☽

Now

"By the time I awoke, it was too late. The cops had found her, and cries of 'Jack the Ripper' were filling the streets," I said flatly, staring at the ring on the table. "I found that in her room...later. I don't know why I took it. She was butchered because of me, I didn't deserve it, but I wanted... I don't know."

I pushed it toward Sam.

She looked like she didn't want to take it.

"I left London later that night. I've never been back."

With a small frown, she picked up the ring and closed her eyes. She was about to learn more about me than she ever wanted to know, but only during the time period where I crossed paths with Mary and onward. At least she wouldn't get all two thousand years.

After several minutes, she put the ring down. "She's telling the truth," she said, but sounded shaky after all she'd seen.

"Why didn't you ever tell the cops anything that you knew?" Morton asked, his lips and brow both pulled down.

"I was an unfortunate," I said, feeling more dead inside than ever. "We weren't much listened to. And I look like a child, even less to be listened to... And if they found out what I was? It would be the end of me. I couldn't risk it."

"You could've tried," Sam said quietly, like she was judging me but didn't want to sound like she was judging me.

"Even if just anonymously, or disappearing after you did… Or recently, when the vampire thing wouldn't be a big deal. All these centuries, people thinking all these things… You should've said something, at some point, before it landed at your doorstep like this."

"You should've tried," Morton agreed.

I sighed and covered my face with my hands. A Tarot card flashed before my eyes. "I know," I whispered, admitting to my greatest shame.

The thing that had haunted me since 1888 and made me twitch every time I heard the phrase 'Jack the Ripper.' The thing that sat on my dead centuries as a weight that I could barely live with.

"I know…"

TRACE

Content Warning: This story involves references to child abuse and the long-term mental/emotional implications of it. (Nothing is written out in any way, however. It is only referenced/hinted at.)

I am...disputed.

Do you know what it's like to have your entire being, your entire identity, be a debate where no one doing the debating is actually listening to you?

I hope you're listening, because I want to tell you about when the walls came tumbling down.

Eve agreed to help me write this and to wrangle the others to flesh it out. I'm told that the writing of it will be therapeutic.

I hope so.

❨○❩

Cassandra

It was really like any other night. There was no way I could have guessed it was a night that would change everything I thought I knew about myself. Not that it all happened at once, because it never happens that way. That night just started the first domino falling in a long line of dominos that would end with me being knocked over.

D and I had a nice room at the Coven House, and our relationship had been progressing well, steadily and rather boring, but I liked that about it. He went to work each night for the Stanton Agency, while I assisted in the managing of the Coven House. I very rarely left the house alone, though. That was for a couple of reasons. My abilities as a vampire healer made me a bit of a magnet for the less controlled of my kind, and then I occasionally had moments where I kind of... faded out. I didn't know what it meant then, and it happened less as the months progressed, so I didn't worry about it. I also didn't want to worry anyone else with it, but it made me nervous to be out alone.

That night, D was at work. I was in my room and using my computer, a laptop that I sat on the bed to use since D's monster desktop took up one whole corner on its own. I was doing some accounting of the house's finances when there was a knock on my door.

"Cassandra, it's Shayna," the Coven House's lead warden called through the door.

Wardens were like the security guards of the house, but being vampires, no one could use so banal a term as 'security guard,' of course.

"Come in," I called back.

She opened the door and stepped in. Tall and solidly built, she was an imposing presence that I had taken a long time just to be comfortable around. Now that I was used to her, it wasn't such a problem and I knew that she had my best interests at heart. She took her duties, and her charges, very seriously.

"You have a visitor," she said in her Israeli accent. "Two, actually. A man named Dane Walker and a girl, Tricia Smith. I checked their IDs and they match. I said I would see if you were willing to meet them."

My whole body tensed at the first name, although I didn't recognize the second. I almost told her that I was not in the least bit willing to come downstairs. Dane Walker was a man that I had no intention of ever seeing again, but a part of me was curious. My time as a vampire had begun to make me stronger, somewhat, and I knew that I could defend myself if I had to. I looked at my computer and closed out the files, then shut the laptop. I stood up like I was preparing myself for battle and nodded at the warden. She eyed me dubiously, no doubt able to read my reticence, but she would not question me.

Without another word, she turned and walked down the hall. I followed her out of my room and down the stairs into the receiving room. It was stiff and formal, but it was where all guests were brought until Shayna approved them to visit deeper in the house, and she was rigorous and slow to give such approval.

There he was. Seated on the green brocade sofa, beside a girl of maybe seventeen that I had never met, was Dane Walker. He didn't look much different than I recalled, disheveled and with an expression that was always vaguely disapproving. He jumped to his feet when he saw me walk in, although his flickering look toward the warden was a wary one.

The girl didn't get up and if he looked vaguely disapproving, there was nothing 'vague' about the disapproval in her face. I couldn't read humans as well as I could vampires, but there was no mistaking the anger that radiated off her. It was so strong that I almost left immediately, but I held my ground.

"Cassie," he said with such familiarity that my skin began to crawl.

"Cassandra," I corrected tightly.

He stopped and nodded slowly. "Cassandra," he said. "It's good to see you. I've been trying to find you for a while, after our...last meeting."

I was unsettled. He was being highly solicitous, and

I wasn't used to that from him. It was disconcerting, and I didn't like that feeling.

"Why?" I asked suspiciously. Shayna remained a lingering, protective presence behind me.

"Why?" he repeated, looking honestly surprised at my question. "Because you're my daughter, of course."

I shook my head. "Not anymore," I said. "That girl is gone."

Now the girl, Tricia, spoke up. Her words dripped with venom that I could read as clearly as anything but didn't understand. She wore heavy eye shadow and liner, but it could do nothing to hide the malice in her brown eyes. When she turned that gaze in my direction, I felt certain it was directed at me. "I told you it was stupid to come here, Dad."

The word 'dad' knocked me back like a physical blow. I had no sister, so he must have re-married and had a stepdaughter. She was so young. It could only have been in the past year, and already she was calling him Father? It didn't make any sense to me, but I knew deep down just how bad news it was.

"Shut up, girl," he snapped at her, and I was reminded of the man I had known, rather than the one he was trying to present now. Strangely, his show of anger helped in a very small way to settle me down again. It was familiar. Still, it was a very small adjustment and not enough to make me in the least bit comfortable.

Tricia didn't say anything further. She just glared daggers at me like I was the one who had snapped.

I heard the deep breath he took before he turned back to me and put on a smile that reminded me of a plastic doll. It was creepy, and I felt myself shaking inwardly again. I almost took a step back, but I caught myself. I reminded myself that I was a grown woman now, and a vampire. I could handle this.

"Why do you stay at this place?" he asked, trying to

sound warm. It didn't work. He glanced at Shayna. "No offense to the lovely establishment," he said to her before turning back to me, "but this isn't your home, darling. You belong with me, in the house you grew up in."

The words 'home' and 'darling' and 'belong' and 'grew up in' all collided in my skull. I felt like my head started to gray out. I tried to keep my wits, but…

Cassie

…my daddy was staring at me in that way. It made me not happy. I tried to step back and get small, but I couldn't. The girl on the couch was my sister. I always wanted a sister, but she didn't look like she liked me. That made me sad.

I always wanted people to like me. I wanted to make people happy.

Daddy stepped toward me. I didn't want him to come closer, but I knew he'd be mad if I said so, so I didn't say anything. I bit my bottom lip and stared at him, trying to think of someplace else I could be.

The door opened. It was the big guy. The one with spiky dark hair and super eyes. His name was D. Not his real name, but everyone called him D. I knew his real name, but it was our secret. Like a pinkie promise, so I wouldn't tell anyone ever. I don't tell secrets that have to stay secret.

As soon as he came into the room, he looked around. He got mad. I knew he didn't like what he saw, but I didn't understand why. He wasn't mad at me. I could tell. He always looked at me really sweet and nice. I liked him. At Daddy, though, he looked real mad. Even though it wasn't at me, his being so mad scared me.

"What *the fuck* are you doing here?!" he roared at my daddy. His voice got real loud as he moved forward. I knew he was real mad 'cause he used the bad word, the really bad word.

"What are you doing here?" Daddy asked. He looked scared. He looked as scared as my friend D looked angry.

D grabbed Daddy by the front of his jacket and threw him almost all out of the room. The girl shrieked, but I didn't understand what she said as she rushed toward Daddy. I didn't want Daddy to be mad, but I didn't want to go to him. I didn't want to be that close to him like she did and was good to stay right here. The tall, scary woman—Ms. Shayna—moved forward to hold D and keep him from jumping on Daddy. He looked like he wanted to hit him, but she stopped him and let Daddy and the girl scramble back. They left really fast.

Seeing them go made me feel funny. My head got fuzzy, and I...

Cassandra

"What..." I stammered as I looked around. My father and stepsister were hurrying out the front door and D was standing in the middle of the room. His shoulders were up in the way they got when he was angry, and I knew how displeased he must have been when he walked into the room and saw them.

I shouldn't have agreed to meet them, I knew, but I couldn't change it now. At least they were gone. He turned to me, the anger fleeing and concern replacing it. I tried to smile at him, but suddenly, I felt nauseated. That was a feeling that I had not felt since I had been turned. It startled and confused me. The room started to spin.

I blacked out.

☾○☽

When I came to, I was laying in bed. Inanely, the first thing I thought was to wonder where my laptop had gone. That thought was very brief-lived as I saw D sitting beside the bed with a very concerned expression. That was when I wondered what had happened, and I remembered blacking out. It must have been something different than the usual, because other times never caused that look on his face.

I turned to him as I opened my eyes further, and he jumped out of the chair and moved closer to me, taking me up in a tight embrace. It was fortunate I didn't need to breathe.

"D," I said with a faint laugh now tinged with worry of my own. "What happened?"

"You passed out," he said simply, letting me go enough to look at my face. "Like, stone cold, you just crumbled to the floor. If my heart still beat, it would've stopped. I realized you were unconscious and brought you to bed."

I frowned. That was very unusual. "Maybe Abby can explain it?" She was the other vampire in the house with healing abilities, although not as strong as mine.

He nodded. "She's already been up. All she could say was that there was something 'weird' going on and we should get a second opinion." D smiled weakly. "I called Sarah, because she's in town." Sarah was a necromancer. She used to be an animator, but her power blossomed into full-blown necromancy a while back. She 'leveled up,' as D and I liked to say. Animators can raise corpses into short-termed zombies. Necromancers have power that extends to all the dead, including vampires.

Luckily, Sarah was on our side.

"She's on her way," D added.

"Alright," I replied, just to show that I was listening and not fading out of the conversation as I sometimes did. I hated to think of all this fuss being around me, but I knew that this was weird. Vampires don't pass out, and then

Abby's pronouncement of 'something weird' had me kind of nervous. I hoped that Sarah would be able to come up with an answer. I didn't want to keep D so worried.

We sat in silence then, since neither of us wanted to give voice to the amorphous worries floating around in both of our minds. It was enough to clear the thought of my father from my head, however, and I wasn't going to complain about that. I didn't understand why he had shown up after all this time, although I supposed I wasn't surprised he wanted me to come home. He had always been displeased when he felt like he was losing control.

Soon, Shayna was again knocking on our door and announcing a visitor. This one was 'Shayna Approved,' so she just let Sarah in.

Tall and lean with short hair and light eyes, Sarah Beaumont walked in with an air of someone in command of herself. She was composed and professional, but she did smile kindly at me as she nodded at the both of us and took the seat D vacated. She asked us what had happened in detail, and we told her. She frowned thoughtfully.

"I don't know if you'll be able to feel this or not," she said, "but I'm going to use my magic on you. It's kind of like a magical physical, but with less hassle."

"Alright," I said with as much smile as I could manage.

She inhaled slowly. As a human, she actually needed to breathe, rather than us vampires who just breathed to speak or out of habit. It started as a tingle that made the hair on my body try to rise. It brought a shiver like from the cold, even as I felt like I should be sweating...if my body had any moisture with which to sweat. She looked placid but intent at first, and then her brows drew down and she looked...confused.

"That can't be," she murmured to herself. The tingling faded for a few moments and then started up again, like she had stopped and restarted her magical 'scan' but at a more intense level than before. I shivered outright but didn't complain. The look on her face made me even more nervous, and I wanted to know what she felt. Finally, just when I thought my teeth might start chattering, she stopped again and sat back.

"What is it?" D asked impatiently.

"I know what I felt, but it's not possible," she said, looking dumbfounded.

"What?" I pressed, feeling almost desperate.

She looked at me and then D and then back at me. "You're...pregnant."

There was a long moment of silence while we all stared at one another.

"I'm what?"

"She's what?"

I knew that our volumes must have jumped a great deal because Sarah winced, but she didn't complain.

My mind raced.

"I'm a vampire, Sarah," I said, like she didn't know. "That's not possible." Every reproductive function I had was turned 'off' when I was turned, and the same for D. Vampires could not reproduce like they could when they were human, so there was just no way that what she said could be true.

"I felt a heartbeat, Cassandra," Sarah said slowly, "and not from your heart. There is a tiny, rapid heartbeat in your womb."

"How..." D said. He was rarely at a loss for words, but right then, he just gaped at her.

Sarah sat back and folded her arms across her chest. Her brows had not unknit since this had begun, and she looked very focused. "On incredibly rare occasions, a vampire man and a human woman have been known to reproduce. When this happens, it creates the dhampir. We know of some from history, but it's always a human woman and always a vampire man who is within roughly a year since he was turned. It's theorized that some…biological matter remains in his system for a variable period of time, leaked during sex. It's so minor that it almost never takes, but again, on that rare time…

"But I have absolutely no idea how a vampire woman possibly could have conceived. You stop ovulating as soon as you die, and vampirism does not bring it back." She sighed roughly and just stared. "I checked twice. There is a child in your body, and it's human. It's alive."

"I'm…pregnant?" I repeated. Even as the words came out of my mouth, I felt like an idiot, because this point had been very strongly made, but I just couldn't process it. I couldn't believe it, because that idea had been given up on at death. In fact, even before that, I had never really thought about or particularly wanted children. Well, it wasn't that I didn't want them, I just didn't pine after one either.

Even so, I was going to have one now. I was pregnant… with a human child.

"I'm going to do some research," she told us, pulling me back out of my thoughts. "I have access to some old tomes now that may give me some kind of answer. In the meantime, I guess I'll kind of be your midwife. I'll come by to check on you often and if anything happens or changes, let me know, okay?"

We nodded, and she excused herself.

D stared at me and then took my face and kissed me. "I don't know whether to be happy or horrified," he admitted, leaning back and running both hands through his hair.

"I don't know either," I said weakly. The room spun slightly…

Anne

"We're going to have a baby!" D exclaimed, holding his hair.

I stared at his look of shock with one of my own. I was going to have a baby? D and I had been together for a while, but I didn't think it would ever happen. We hadn't been using any sort of protection, after all, so we must have been trying to conceive. I knew he must have been losing hope too, looking as startled as he was.

"That's wonderful!" I said, smiling.

"Really?" he asked, pulling back. "A minute ago, you said you didn't know if you were horrified or not."

"Horrified?" I said. I couldn't remember saying anything like that. "Why would I be horrified? A baby is a wonderful thing."

He pulled his hands away from his head and took both of mine, looking very seriously into my eyes. I couldn't understand his solemnity. Wasn't he happy about this? I couldn't understand why he looked that way.

Now he nodded slowly. "It is, but we don't know how it happened or how it's going to go, with the vampire thing. I thought you'd be concerned."

I blinked. Vampire thing? What was he talking about now? "Don't be foolish," I said, brushing it off with a laugh and shake of my head. "The vampire thing," I repeated, thinking that he must be making a joke at my expense. Frankly, it seemed like really bad timing to be making such an outlandish joke.

"Cassandra, what's going on?" He touched my forehead and temple. "This must be quite the shock."

"D, I don't—"

Eve

I couldn't let that continue.

Although Anne was entirely unaware of what had happened, I wrestled physical control away before she went too far. Of all the personalities, Anne was the one who still refused to accept that we were no longer human. It had been a little while now and on those very rare times she popped out, she wouldn't hear anything of it.

If she was allowed to speak too much, she would bring too many questions down on us, and I couldn't let Cassandra be put through that. I loved her too much. She was such a sweet woman and had been through so much. Well, we all had, but she was where it started. And now the poor thing was so overwhelmed that she just couldn't be out, and since none of the others could handle the moment, it was up to me to take over.

Have you figured us out yet? You will.

I smiled at D and leaned into his hand. He had remarkable anger issues at times, but he was so gentle with Cassandra. He loved her a great deal, even if there were things he didn't know. It wasn't that she was hiding anything, because she didn't really know either.

"It was a shock," I said, working to fix the damage that Anne had done. "Who could ever have expected this? I'm sure Sarah will figure something out, though. And so will we. D, we're going to have a baby, and a living one. That's a good thing, isn't it?"

I could see his whole being change with what I said. Now that I was seeing it as a good thing and was confident that everything would be okay, so was he. The boy was so connected with Cassandra, it was rather sweet and beautiful. It was always clear how much they needed each other, and I have always been so happy for my girl that she found him, even if he had his issues. Don't we all?

Leaning forward, I hugged him. Sometimes, I felt a little guilty when I was affectionate with him. I worried that if he knew about me, he'd feel like he was cheating on her, or she'd feel that way if she knew too. It couldn't be helped, though. I had to do what I had to do to keep her together. That was my whole existence.

He hugged me back, tight, and I rested my head on his broad shoulder. "We're going to have a baby," he whispered in my ear.

I smiled. I knew that it couldn't possibly be easy for Cassandra, but I was happy for her. I was sure that this was going to be a good thing.

❨O❩

Not all vampires dream during their daylight comas, but Cassandra does. Maybe it's the influence of Anne and her resistance, or maybe it's just that my girl is special. Either way, she dreams and often remembers it. If she doesn't, one of the others will. And I do, because I always do. Nothing happens that I'm not aware of.

That's what being the Trace is all about.

Over the hours of daylight that day, which were few because the days were still pretty short so early in the year, she dreamed of many things. There was a lot about babies, as you would expect, but she also dealt with the emotions seeing her bastard of a father brought up in her. She didn't remember everything he'd done to her, but I did.

That's why I could hardly blame her when in her dreams, she killed him.

Cassandra

When dark was falling, I woke up before D as I always did, but he wasn't too far behind.

Last night was fuzzy, but I had the feeling of being happy.

I felt like I'd gotten over some of the shock and instead was happy about the news. That was good, because it was good news. I was pretty sure. It was kind of a miracle, I guess. I trusted Sarah to help take good care of me. She was a good friend of D's, because he had been her bodyguard while she was still an animator for the Stanton Agency and so they'd gotten close. I didn't know her as well, but I trusted her because he did.

He started stirring beside me, and I rolled onto my side. I was smiling at him as he woke, groaning and grunting as he stubbornly relented to consciousness.

"You are not an evening person," I teased.

"Nope," he chuckled, stretching before turning to face me as well. "How are you feeling?"

I suddenly had a strong feeling that I was going to be hearing that a lot for a few months, and then after too. I would just have to get used to it. I knew he asked because he loved me, so I leaned forward and kissed him. "I'm fine," I assured him. "It's still a lot to take in, but it'll all be fine. I'm fine."

He smiled and kissed me, and then did a little more to me, and I did a little more to him, before we both got up, showered, and he dressed to go to work.

I went downstairs a little while after. When I did, Jade came out of her office and gestured for me to join her. I blinked, wondering what this was about as I walked into the room after her.

Jade is the leader of our coven. If she has a last name, she's never chosen to tell anyone, and no one ever asks.

"Please, have a seat," she said, gesturing at one of the large armchairs. I sat in one and she sat in the other. They were both large and elegant, as was the dark wood table that sat between them. She poured tea into two fine, china cups and handed one to me. I looked at it and knew instantly that there was blood in it. I wondered at how that worked, but I wasn't going to ask. "How are you feeling?"

I realized then that she must have known. I wasn't sure how, but she had to. "I'm fine, thank you." I lifted the cup and took a sip. It was warm, like it had come from the vein. It tasted different than when something had been heated in the microwave, or just drunk cold.

She smiled in an economical gesture of expression, just enough to make her point. "I am sure you have guessed that I've heard your news," she said what I had just been thinking. "It must be quite a shock, but it is amazing. Congratulations."

"Thank you," I said again, bowing my head. I couldn't imagine she just called me into her office to congratulate me, because that wasn't her style. She was polite and proper, but she wasted little effort. There was more coming, so I just had to wait for it.

She sipped her own tea and then set the cup down, settling back into her chair. She looked small in that large chair, and yet her presence managed to dominate the room quite easily.

"This would make quite the change to your circumstances, becoming three instead of two," she began. "I know that you only just learned, and I am aware that…things can happen." She was never one to mince words or reality. I didn't want to think about those 'things' though, so I didn't. "But you will want to start thinking about your future, I'm sure."

"Yes, of course," I said, nodding slowly. "I do think we have a little time for that."

"Certainly," she agreed, "but it never hurts to start thinking. This is a human child, so one such thing to consider will be if you wish to remain here in the Coven House."

The dreadful idea suddenly occurred to me that she might want to kick me out of the house because of the baby, and this was her polite, proper way of leading up to it. I felt this rush of panic that might have stopped my heart, if it beat. As it was, I stared at her with growing fear, and my head began to get fuzzy.

Her next words cleared it, though. "You and D and your child are, of course, most welcome to remain here. We can arrange another room, and I am sure that Shayna will extend any possible protections such a unique child would need," she continued. The world stopped going gray, and my panic eased. "I just want you to consider that it's what you want. We would need to arrange someone to be part of the household during the daylight hours. We have the daytime warden, but he is not qualified for nanny work."

She had clearly thought this through more than I had already, but she was good at what she did. Jade was always a good leader and one who thought clearly and completely. Vampires that survive through so many centuries have to be. Stupidity rarely manages to do that for our kind. Or most any kind, except humanity...

"Thank you," I said again. I was saying that a lot, it seemed. "I will speak with D, and we shall consider all the options, but I find it hard to imagine we will want to leave here. This is our home."

"We would be glad to have it so," she assured me. "But we would also understand if you wished a new situation."

Concluding our conversation, I left her office. Twenty-four hours had treated me like an emotional yoyo. Although I could not sleep like a human, I could still feel fatigue and was feeling it pretty strongly then. I considered just going back up to the bedroom and lying down, maybe playing around on the computer at something that wasn't too mentally demanding.

As I passed the window, I happened to look out. Just at the edge of the streetlamp's cone of light, I thought I saw a car. It looked familiar, like my father's, but since no one had come up to the door, I figured it couldn't be him, right?

Right?

Cassie

I didn't see Daddy anywhere. Maybe it wasn't him. I hoped it wasn't him, because I didn't want to talk to him. I didn't want to see him at all, so I left the window. I went downstairs to see the other kid in the house. She was older than me, but nice...most of the time.

Going down into the basement, I held tight to the rail because I had to be safe, and stairs could be scary. The basement was always dark, but I walked real careful till I got to the bottom and went straight to Abby's door. I knocked and called her name. After a moment, she called back and said I could come in.

She was sitting on the floor and looked at me. Her look was funny sometimes and made me feel weird. "Right," she said. I didn't understand why she said it, but I didn't ask.

"Uhm," I began nervously. "I was wondering if I could play with the pretty cards?"

"Of course," she said. The weird look went away, and she moved to take out the deck of cards with the pretty pictures, handing them to me.

Cassandra

My head cleared, and I found myself sitting in the living room.

I couldn't remember moving from the window to the couch, but I obviously had. Since there wasn't anyone hovering anxiously around me, I could assume that this was just one of my usual foggy moments and not whatever had happened the other night. Everything was quiet, so I got up and was heading upstairs when the door opened.

D walked in. He smiled when he saw me and came close to give me a kiss. "How are you feeling?"

"How many times a night are you going to ask me that?" I said with a soft laugh.

"More and more," he replied unabashedly. "I'm not gonna get too close right now because I got some grave dirt. One of the zombies tonight went tumbling into me, losing its mojo before Lucia expected it to. I caught it, unintentionally. I've got to go take a shower." He kissed me again and then went upstairs.

I had to laugh again, thinking how strange life had become and how it was only going to get stranger from there. Although I had been planning to go upstairs, I decided to go to the kitchen again. I hadn't gotten two steps when I heard a car door shut outside. I went to the window and saw someone. It took a moment, but I recognized the someone. Letting D see him again was a bad idea, so I hurried outside to make him go away.

In doing so, I wasn't really thinking that clearly. I just knew that I had to make him leave.

"What are you doing here?" I exclaimed. "Didn't we make it very clear before that you are not welcome here?"

"How can I be unwelcome here?" he said without any of the shame he should have. "You are my daughter, Cassie, you belong with me. You don't belong here in this...freak show."

"Freak show?" I repeated with horror. My fangs dropped, and my lips pulled back over the words as I said them, "Sure I do." Even as I felt anger about what he said about my home and my new family, I took a step back. He saw my retreat and clearly felt it was an advantage, like I was scared of him. It made him bold enough to ignore the teeth and push forward.

"Come on, Cassie. You're still my little girl. Come home." He held his hand out to me, fingertips almost close enough to brush my clothing—

Andrew

"Get the fuck away from her!" I exploded.

I smacked his hand away and was rewarded with the sound of flesh cracking against flesh, vampire strength overcoming human frailty.

I didn't stop. I took a big step forward and pushed him as hard as I could.

He would hurt Cass. I couldn't let him do that.

I couldn't let him ever hurt Cass again. Hadn't he done enough?

"You bastard!" I hissed between the fangs. I loved those things. He was on his ass on the cold, hard ground from where I had shoved him. I stood over him, considering whether I should pick him up to punch him again or kick him.

"What's wrong with you?" he exclaimed.

"What's wrong with *me*?" I cried. "You sick fuck ask what's wrong with me?" I pulled my foot back to—

Eve

—the muscles in my leg trembled as I kept Andrew from kicking him. We didn't need an assault on our hands, and Andrew would kill him if I didn't intervene. I forced the foot back onto the ground and took a step back.

Dane got to his feet, shaking with rage now clear on his face.

"Cassandra Anne Walker," he declared in a fatherly tone of authority that he had absolutely no right to use. "You will come home."

"No," I said and started to—

Andrew

"Fuck you!" I shouted. The world was gray, fading in and out, but he was still in front of me and that was all that mattered. "You won't ever get her again!" I started forward—

Eve

—I pulled him back. My body shook all over with the effort.

"Just leave," I managed to say.

Dimly, I was aware of a door shutting.

I blacked out. We all blacked out.

☾O☽

It is not possible to describe the fear I felt upon waking. I didn't black out. I never left Cassandra, not like the others. That wasn't my role. I was the one who had to stay on top of everything, but I had blacked out. There wasn't anyone who could make me do that, or so I had always thought...

Opening my eyes, I felt sore. I realized I was on the ground. I had collapsed, again. I had blacked out twice and fallen to the ground like refuse. What was going on? Panic rushed through me as I started to push myself up, but if it was bad at that moment, the next was all the worse.

Lying on the ground just a few feet away was Cassandra's father. He was clearly dead, because a vampire knows dead. He was covered in blood, facing away from me. I screamed. I couldn't help it. The sound was high and shrill, probably echoing through the entire town with a vampire's magic and vocal cords. The sound lasted as long as the small amount of breath in my lungs would let it, stopped for me to gasp, and then I did it again.

This was bad. This was very bad.

The door to the house behind me opened, and I heard people rushing out. I couldn't even turn around so it wasn't until they were right in front of me that I knew who it was. Jade, Shayna, and D. Of course.

D was right in front of me, grabbing my face in his hands and holding me close. "What happened?" he asked, but there was a buzzing in my ears.

"I don't know!" I cried earnestly. "I saw him and came out to tell him to leave and then…I blacked out again." I had no tears with which to cry, but the sound of tears was in my voice. "I woke up and saw him…"

"We have to call the cops," Jade said. I couldn't tell if she was talking to me or Shayna, but it didn't matter. I knew she was right, even if I wanted to argue. I didn't want the cops to come because I knew how this looked. There was a dead body that wouldn't get up again and a dead body next to it that was the only thing around that moved.

It looked like I had killed someone, and I couldn't remember a damn thing. Even I couldn't hang on then.

Cassandra

I was sitting on the doorstep with D beside me when the cop cars showed up. There was the coroner's van with the assistant medical examiner. I had been lucky enough to not have met him on any professional basis until now. I had been able to piece together some things but knew I couldn't remember everything. There was a big hole in my mind around what had happened, and I tried to figure out if I could have killed someone while blacked out.

There was dirt on me, so I knew that I'd been on the

ground...so I'd collapsed again, but was that before or after he'd died?

He was my father. I should have felt sad, maybe, but I didn't. I was just scared and foggy.

D had his arm around me as I hugged myself, leaning into him. I watched as the crime scene technicians started moving around like someone had kicked over an ant hill, searching the immediate area. Some asked Jade if they could search the house, and she reluctantly agreed. No one talked to me until Vance and Sam showed up, but they all looked at me.

"Alright, so, what happened?" Vance asked. He was a vampire too and he knew me, but he was a cop. He had to be a cop. I wished I could get favorable treatment, but I knew I couldn't ask for it.

"The dead man is my father," I said, feeling flat and defeated. "We are...estranged, you could say. He showed up, and I came outside to tell him to leave. I didn't want to see him, but he was stubborn. I got upset and then...I blacked out. I woke up on the ground, I know, but it's still kind of foggy. They say inside that I screamed like hell and they rushed out."

Sam was the one making notes, although Vance was the one who continued talking. "Do you have any reason to kill him?"

Yes. "I guess, maybe," I admitted weakly. "If he wouldn't leave. He could be a very...pushy man. He didn't like to take no for an answer and always pushed until he...he got what he wanted." I felt the edges of my mind growing fuzzy again, but I fought it.

"The victim was stabbed," Vance went on. "Do you own a knife?"

"No," I said. "I mean, the Coven House has some for cutting stuff up, but I don't own any personally." A throbbing pain began in my head, and everything was dim. The stress of this was overwhelming, but I knew that I couldn't just leave. I wanted to leave. I wanted to run away from it all, but I knew that I couldn't. I looked guilty enough already, though I was sure...I thought I was sure...that I hadn't killed him.

"Did you kill him?" Vance asked plainly.

Something about the bluntness of the question overwhelmed me, and I...

Eve

Andrew tried to come out, but he'd land us in prison for sure. He probably would confess if I let him. Even my awareness stayed foggy with him wrestling for control. I knew that he wanted to protect her. As much as I was the memory keeper, he was the protector. In this case, however, I was pretty sure it would have the opposite effect.

"I suppose blacking out makes me unable to answer with the surety I would like," I said, more calmly than Cassandra had been managing. I saw in their faces that they recognized it, but I had to keep calm. If I lost control again, I might black out a second time tonight or Andrew could take over. "But I'm as certain as I can be that I didn't do it. You said he was stabbed, and I don't carry a blade. Was he bitten?"

"No," Vance said with a shake of his head. "He wasn't bitten, and his neck wasn't broken."

Those were a vampire's favored methods of killing. Stabbing was odd. I looked down at myself and my hands, and I didn't see any blood. That would work in Cass's favor, I was pretty sure, or at least so I hoped.

"You really can't remember anything after coming outside?" Sam asked.

"No," I said sadly, looking up at her. "I don't like it any more than you do, Detective, I can promise you."

Sam nodded. "I'm sure." She exchanged a look with Vance and then moved off to talk to some of the gathered uniforms. Vance stayed. "This looks bad, Cass. You have to know that, but there's as much that suggests it might not be you as it might be. We won't be arresting you at this time, but you're going to be under suspicion. Be clear on that, and don't go anywhere."

I smiled weakly. "I don't plan to. I assure you."

He nodded and then also moved off. I sat with D and watched the commotion. When I couldn't take it anymore, I turned my head and leaned into him. He urged me to my feet, and I rose obediently, barely able to think for myself at that point. He took me up to our room and got me to lie down. Then, he lied down beside me and just held me while I felt my focus waving in and out. I closed my eyes and just held on.

Before I knew it, the cops left and dawn came.

Cassandra

D didn't want to go to work the next night, but I told him that he should. He only agreed if I promised to call should there be anything. He left, and I stayed in my room. I didn't want to face the world right then, it was all just too much. I felt like I was hanging on by a thread as it was. The chances of finding the scissors that would cut that thread went up very quickly if I stepped out of this room, so I didn't intend to do so.

A little while into the night, Shayna announced that I had a guest. Before I panicked, though, she told me it was Sarah, and I relaxed. She came in and smiled at me, pulling up the chair beside the bed.

"I heard," she said simply, not explaining and not needing to. "Are you holding up alright? I can't imagine the stress of that on top of the shock you already had." She held her hand out, and I put mine into it. I appreciated that her gesture was a request, rather than just touching me. D was the only one allowed to do that.

"As well as can be expected, I suppose," I said honestly, but without getting into any more detail than that. It wasn't that I distrusted Sarah, but I didn't want to talk about it.

She accepted my answer with a nod. "I came by to check up on you, another little magical scan. You'll be seeing a lot of me, so I can keep an eye on things. I still have no idea how you became pregnant or, honestly, how you're sustaining it, but you are. There is a heartbeat, which means you're at least six weeks. From the strength of it, I'm betting you're further along than that. With a little study, I may be able to learn more…but right now, I'm just confused.

"You're not alive. Your body should not be able to keep a human fetus alive, but it is, and I'm not a fan of that changing so I'll do all that I can to make sure it stays that way." She smiled again and gently squeezed my hand. "Be aware that I don't believe you will be able to deliver, so you'll be looking at a c-section. At least with your vampire healing, however, you'll recover much faster than human women do."

I nodded slowly, trying to take all that in. In my shock from the idea that I couldn't get pregnant, it didn't really dawn on me that I shouldn't be able to sustain a child either. That was an abruptly terrifying thought. I might not have wanted a baby, but I didn't want to lose the life that was now inside me. The idea of the caesarean section didn't really bother me at all, just the idea that my body could…starve the child, in essence. How was I going to make sure that didn't happen?

Then something equally frightening: would I end up doing this all in prison?

Unaware of my inner turmoil, Sarah was continuing, "I'm going to take a look over you now." After I nodded, I felt the tingling start. I leaned back and closed my eyes, just letting her do what she would do. "The heartbeat is strong.

I think I can almost make out the feeling of...separation between you two. It's hard to explain, but I think my magic is starting to feel the separate entities."

"So, it's still okay?"

"Yes, it's fine," she said with a small smile. "The rest of you is feeling a bit...rough, but I think that's understandable."

I frowned slightly. "Rough?"

She nodded slightly. "I can feel a... There's discordance in you. A vampire is a magical being, when all is said and done, and I can feel shifts in that magic. I feel that in you, but you're under a lot of stress and your body is going through something that the vampire magic wasn't meant to handle. So, it's going to be strange."

I supposed that made sense, so I nodded. "All right, thank you, Sarah."

She bid me good night and headed out. I settled back into bed, but my head was a mess now. I thought, what if I lost the baby? What about delivery? What about if I went to prison for killing my father? What if... What if...

Then, as one might expect, my brain shifted to my dad. Some part of me kept saying I should grieve, because he was my father, but I just couldn't. He had done things to me that no father should. I couldn't really remember it all, but I knew that those things had happened, and I knew what they made me feel. I tried to stop thinking about them, but it was hard. My brain was apparently out of my control, and—

Eve

That had to stop. We existed to keep her from going down that road, after all.

The girl had too much on her mind. She wasn't going to be able to handle it all. I loved her, she was me and birthed me, but I knew better than anyone possibly could just how fragile she was. The pregnancy was hard enough, but this stuff with her father being killed... That was just too much. That alone would have been too much. That man had no place in her life. I knew that better than even she did.

We had to know what had happened. I still couldn't remember, and that frustrated and scared me to no end. Even during her daylight coma, I was aware of what was going on. How could I black out?

We needed answers. Cassandra was a suspect, so they weren't going to tell her anything more than they already had, and I suspected that Vance Johnston may have already told her more than he should have. The only people to really know what had happened were us and her father and the killer, assuming one of us wasn't... No. I just couldn't believe that. We couldn't have killed him. Andrew couldn't force me to black out, and he was the only one violent enough to kill someone.

On a whim, I decided to go see my stepsister. She might be able to provide insight into the man we hadn't known for over a year. That had been with good reason, but maybe some information about him would shed light on possibilities. I could recall hearing a door shut before I lost consciousness, so maybe someone else had been there and maybe finding out more about him could tell me who.

I managed to slip out of the house without Shayna knowing. Cassandra didn't know her routines well enough to do so, but I did.

Of course, I didn't have a car of my own, so I walked. The Coven House is in a fairly remote area of the city, but a vampire can move pretty quickly. I hadn't forgotten the way to my childhood home just outside of town and arrived there a little over an hour and a half later. I saw only one car in the driveway. My father's had been towed away from the Coven House. Something about it caught my attention, but I couldn't place what it was, so I walked up to the door instead.

I felt...nervous about what I was doing there, but I knew it needed to happen. I lifted my hand and knocked.

A few moments later, Tricia opened the door. Hate immediately filled her gaze, and she started to slam the door without saying anything, but I caught it.

"Please, I just want to talk," I said quickly.

"There is absolutely nothing that we have to talk about," she spat, turning and going back into the house. I knew I wasn't welcome, but I followed her anyway. I noticed that the house wasn't quite as squalid as it had been the last time I was here, but it was still a mess. I shut the door behind me and contained my revulsion for being there.

"Please, Tricia," I said, holding out my hands. "I didn't kill him."

She spun around on her heel and folded her arms across her chest. She had a small frame and wasn't wearing as much makeup now. "How would you even know?" she sneered. "You blacked out."

I felt snapped back. "How do you know that?"

Her lips pursed. "The cops told me when they came to talk to me," she said with a shrug that was intended to feign casualness but didn't quite hit the mark. "I still don't have shit to say to you, Miss Perfect."

"What?" She caught me off-guard again. The ground felt like it was staying unsteady, and I couldn't catch my balance. "I don't..." I caught myself and took a breath just as a way to keep myself focused. "Where's your mom?"

"Dead." Her voice was flat, but more venom poured into her gaze. I didn't realize that had even been possible, but she was clearly an overachiever. I almost took a step back from the force of it. "Daddy was the only thing I have, and he didn't even..." She trailed off and looked away.

Her mother was dead, so it was just her and her stepfather. I flashed back to when my own mother died when

I was six, and all that followed. I shuddered. "Why do you mourn him?" I asked. I couldn't help myself at that point. "If you knew what that man did—"

Her violence caught me by surprise. She surged forward the few steps between us and pushed me hard in the chest. It reminded me of the way Andrew pushed Dane, and I felt my protector trying to come out. My world became gray around the edges, but I held him back as she screamed "shut up" at me, over and over. "Bitch" was in there a few times, too.

"I..." I stammered, but I just couldn't. I couldn't handle her and fight Andrew back at the same time. I staggered backward out of the house and ran.

◖O◗

D was sitting on the front step of the Coven House when I walked up. He leaped to his feet the moment he saw me and rushed to me. First he took me in his arms and hugged me so tightly that I would've suffocated as a human. Then he stepped back, still holding my arms, and I saw the anger in his face.

"Where have you been?!" he demanded. "I was worried sick! I thought you said you'd call if something happened!"

"Nothing happened," I assured him. I was glad that Cassandra wasn't out, but Andrew tried to come out again. I had managed to calm him on the walk back, but now he was rearing at the gates again. I pushed him away. "I just needed air. It's so stressful, honey, and I needed to just clear my head." That was kind of true, really. "I promise, nothing happened." That definitely wasn't true, but I knew he'd blow a gasket if I told him that I'd gone to see my crazy step-sister. I knew the cops wouldn't be too thrilled either, but hopefully they wouldn't find out.

He seemed to relax a little, but he still looked dubious.

"So you're okay?"

I put on the best comforting smile I could while I battled for control of this brain and body, stepping forward and embracing him. I pressed my head to his shoulder. "I'm fine," I told him. "Everything is okay. I just needed a little air, but I'm good now." I stifled my sigh. I definitely wasn't good. I was failing Cassandra. "I don't know I ever want to come out again," I whispered.

If he thought the use of the word "come" instead of "go" was odd, he didn't say anything.

Cassandra

I opened my eyes with that fuzzy feeling again, but I was still lying on the bed so maybe it wasn't anything. Although I realized soon after that I wasn't alone. I was laying with my head on D's chest and wondered when he got home, but I knew that it would be stupid to ask. I lifted my head to look up at him.

"Just promise me you won't go out again without telling anybody, okay?" he asked, very seriously. "Not while you're in this condition or with this…murder stuff."

"Out?" I asked before I could stop myself.

His brows knit, and he stroked my cheek. Concern was very plain in his face, and I knew that he was already worried enough as it was. I felt bad for adding to it and wished that I had caught my tongue before it asked the question. "Yeah, to…clear your head."

I nodded quickly. "Right, yeah, I promise I won't go out again without telling anyone."

He still looked at me oddly. I forced a weak smile but dropped my head to his chest again so he wouldn't see the strained, fearful expression in my eyes. Was I really and truly going crazy? Everyone said I was a little 'odd,' and more than once. Was it more than just a bad memory and odd quirks?

I chewed on my lip as I felt D's arms tighten around me. What kind of a mother was I going to make if I was crazy? It was probably just all the stress, right? That had to be it, which meant that once we cleared it all up—if we cleared it all up—I would get better, and everything would be okay. It had to be, because I couldn't contemplate the alternative.

Eve

The girl's dreams were dark that day. They often were, unfortunately, but they were even darker than usual. Way darker than usual. They were so bad that I didn't want her to remember them and I didn't even let her wake up right when the sun went down. I kept control. It was rare that I had to do that, and it bothered me. I was worried about her. I was more worried than I had ever been, and admittedly, that was saying something.

D woke up not long after us. He spent a while assuring himself that I was okay and that I wasn't going to go out without telling anyone before he finally agreed to go to work. I laid on the bed as he took his shower and dressed. I smiled and kissed him good-bye. My mind was in a torrent. I was blacking out. I was having to fight the others for control. Neither of those things had ever happened before, and it couldn't be a good sign.

It was time for a bold stroke. A terrifyingly bold stroke.

I got up and got dressed. As per my promise to D, I told Shayna that I was going out, although I didn't tell her where.

I walked to the police station.

At the desk, I asked for Vance and Sam. The officer there called up, and Vance came down to meet me.

"What are you doing here, Cassandra?" he asked, looking almost suspicious, almost concerned. He gently touched my shoulder to guide me to follow him, which I did, and he led me to an interview room. The blank, pale walls made me nervous, but I endured.

"I need to talk to you two," I said slowly.

He looked at me for a long moment and then nodded. He stepped out to gesture Sam inside with us, and we all sat down. I wished the station would have the type of blood tea that Jade had, but I bet that stuff was expensive and hard to find. So I sat straight, folded my hands, and stared at them as I rested them against the table.

"I have to tell you something, but it's going to be hard for you to believe," I told them very plainly. I forced my eyes up and looked at each detective in turn. Their expressions were wary, and I couldn't blame them. "I know that it will be, but I am begging you to listen with open minds, because it will be the truth."

"We're living in a world where vampire is a legitimate option on an employment form," Sam said with a half-smile. "I'm willing to go on a little faith here. Please, just tell us what you need to. We'll go from there."

My return smile was feeble but genuine. "Thank you, Detective. You're a good woman."

Everyone fell silent and waited for me to begin. I felt like I was going to cry, even though I knew I couldn't. "My name is Eve." Those four words tumbled out of my mouth and I didn't try to stop them because I knew it was now or never. What I was going to say had never been said, never been shown into the light of day, but I knew now that it had to be. "Cassandra is a damaged woman. Her mind is fractured. Her father was a bastard of the first order. He abused her in more ways than I care to count, and her gentle soul couldn't handle it. Her mind broke into pieces."

"Wait," Sam said, holding up her hand. "Are we talking, like, Sybil here?"

"Yes, although I know that her story has been disputed in the decades since as being planted in her mind by her therapist. I can't know the truth of that, but I know the truth of Cassandra. I've been with her since it began. I'm the Trace."

"The what?" This was Vance.

"I'm what psychology has termed the Trace, which is the one personality—not the main, or original—that knows everything. I've been with her since the first moment she broke apart, and I've protected her mind. Aside from Cassandra and I, there are three others."

They were staring at me. I knew this was a lot to take in, and I wished that I could make it easier. I wished that I could just tear open Cassandra's forehead and let them see it for the truth that it was.

"Cassie is still six, which was when it started. Andrew is her protector. Anne is the newest split, the newest alter. She came when Cassandra was turned. She still refuses to accept that Cassandra is a vampire at all," I continued.

"You're right," Vance said with a faint smile. "This is… hard to take in, but stranger things have happened. Why are you telling us now, though? Knowing this sets you up even more strongly as a suspect."

I bit my lip and nodded. "I am aware, but I am also certain that Cassandra didn't do it. Yes, even I blacked out when she did, but we hit the ground. Andrew protects her, but he can't make me black out. If he had done something to her father, I would know. But the present stress is making her black out so entirely that even I don't know things, but the blackouts are true. She just collapses. She couldn't have killed him. I'm sure of it."

Vance and Sam exchanged a long look. "We did find a knife," he admitted. "In the woods beside the road. The blade was covered in his blood, and there was one set of fingerprints. We were actually going to call you tonight to compare them."

Eagerly, I held my hands out. "Please!" I almost cried. My voice was thick. "I'm here to protect Cassandra. This has to end. She can't have this lingering over her head or she'll fracture more. The switches are happening more often now. I'm struggling to control the others in a way I never have. Please." I pushed my hands toward them.

Vance took my hands and lowered them to the table. "We will," he said.

"Have you talked to his stepdaughter?" I asked after a moment. "I..." I grimaced because I didn't want to admit this. "I talked to her last night. I know, I shouldn't have, but I wanted answers. I thought maybe if I knew more about Cassandra's father then I could understand who might have done it. She is angry, and she *hates* Cassandra. I got the impression she was almost..." I hesitated, trying to find the word. "She seemed almost jealous of her. When I began to refer to what Dane had done, she pushed me and screamed at me. I left fast."

Someone knocked on the door. The sound startled me. I jumped slightly but then sunk down as I realized what it was.

Sam got up. A uniformed officer at the door. Nodding at us, she stepped outside, and I realized that Vance's hands were still on mine. He gently squeezed them and then let go.

"Multiple Personality Disorder?" he asked. He sounded dubious but not disbelieving.

"They call it Dissociative Identity Disorder now, I believe," I said weakly. "Many psychiatrists no longer believe it's even a disorder now, just something planted in the mind of patients or used as an excuse to get out of a crime. Personally, I never understood why people couldn't believe that the human mind might protect itself this way. I suppose my perspective is almost...unique. It's rare, but I know for sure that it's possible. Cassandra and I have managed to keep it pretty under control...until now."

He nodded just as the door opened and Sam stepped

back inside. Now she had a folder in her hand. "We got an ID on both the fingerprints and the tire tracks behind the victim's car," she announced. "The tracks belong to a two thousand seven Toyota Camry—"

"There's a car like that at Cassandra's father's house!" I interrupted in surprise.

"Yes," she said with a small smile. "The prints match the stepsister. She was busted for shoplifting two years ago."

"*She* killed him?" I repeated, almost dumbly. "But she was so… She seemed so attached."

"I'm not a psychologist," Sam said, "but this is pretty solid place to start, and to suggest that you are not the one. I'm glad you came in, though. This should move matters off from over your head, and maybe you can get some help." She turned to Vance. I sat, staring numbly. Through the dim, I could hear her tell Vance that uniforms had gone to pick her up.

They seemed to sense that I wasn't all there anymore and left me alone. Vance just said, "You can go when you're ready," before stepping out.

It was a while before I was ready. Had I just spilled the biggest secret of our existence for nothing? No, Sam was right. This couldn't go on like this any longer. I got up and stepped out. As I did, I saw them bringing in Tricia. She was in handcuffs. When she saw me, she started throwing herself around and fighting against the grip of the two officers who were leading her.

"You bitch!" she shrieked, trying to get to me. "You ruined everything! He couldn't let go of *you*! Daddy's fucking favorite! What about me? I was right there! Why didn't I ever measure up against perfect you?! I was right there—" They pulled her away and into a room where I couldn't hear or see her. Andrew wanted to go after her, but I pushed him back.

However, the moment was too much. The idea that she

wanted... I couldn't. I passed out.

Cassandra

I opened my eyes and was in my bed in the Coven House. From my window, I knew that it was far past sunset, but I couldn't remember waking up. Where had the time gone? What had happened to me?

D was sitting on the edge of the bed. I could only see him in profile. He wasn't turned away from me, but he wasn't exactly turned toward me either. The look on his face had me instantly worried. My first thought was that I'd blacked out again, just hadn't woken up, and that maybe something was wrong with the baby...but I didn't see Sarah there. Wouldn't she have been called if that was the case?

"What happened?" I asked. I pushed myself up to a seat and realized that I felt like hell.

"Vance told me," he said quietly. He was still looking down at his hands clasped before him, not at me.

I moved forward and put my hand on his shoulder. "Vance told you what?" I asked. I hadn't seen Vance that night. Had he talked to D about something? Was it about the murder and maybe news? Oh no, maybe it had been bad news and that was why he looked like that. "Please, tell me."

His dark brows were knit heavily as he turned his head to look at me. "You went to the police station tonight and talked to the cops," he told me.

Frowning, I shook my head. "N-no, I didn't."

"You honestly don't remember, do you?" he asked. His voice was soft and so strange, and his expression was so strange. I'd never seen him like this before and frankly, it was scaring the hell out of me.

"Please, tell me what's going on," I whispered.

So he did.

I had blacked out at the police station and Vance had brought me home, which was when he had told D what I had told them.

When he told me, I didn't believe him…at first. I was shocked. It couldn't be real, could it? Things like that didn't happen… Then I started thinking it through, and I realized that it made some things make a lot more sense. I still didn't want to believe it, because that made me beyond insane, but… It made sense. And I didn't believe that Vance and D would be lying to me, so I had said all this, or my mouth had at least.

"Why didn't you ever tell *me*?" The hurt was plain in his voice, and it cut me down to my core, but I hadn't even known.

"I didn't know. And I…couldn't make decisions as this… Eve?" I felt like I was suffocating, but I didn't know what on. "I didn't know. Please, believe me, I would never have kept such a secret from you. I love you." The idea that he might finally decide I was too crazy for him made me shudder.

He seemed to sense my thoughts and finally turned toward me, pulling me into his embrace and holding me close. "It's just…a shock."

I laughed mirthlessly, more like a choking sound. "You're telling me."

When he released me, I just lay back on the bed and curled up into a ball and didn't move for the rest of the night. I couldn't find any more words. He stayed with me, held me, and spoke to me. I couldn't find it in me to reply any more or do any more.

Yet, oddly, I remained me and didn't black out or even go fuzzy. That seemed like some kind of joke.

☾O☽

"It makes sense, actually," Abby said after I told her.

The three of us were sitting in her basement room. D had been glued to me since the night before, even taking the night off from work. I wondered if he wasn't going to find a way to have us surgically connected at this point.

"There were times you acted like a little kid, and sometimes when you damn near tore my head off for saying the 'vampire' word," she went on in her blunt way. She tilted her head. "You know, maybe that explains it too."

Neither D nor I said anything, thinking she would continue, but she didn't. She could be like that sometimes. It was irritating, but I appreciated that she had been pretty nice to me since moving in. She wasn't very kind to most, so I still felt somewhat indebted to her for her care. I now felt it even more so, if I had been this crazy the whole time and she was still my friend.

"Explains what?" D prompted with impatience.

"The pregnancy," she said, looking between us like we should get it. When our obviously vacant looks said we didn't, she rolled her eyes and continued, "You have a personality who refused to acknowledge you were a vampire. The brain and the mind are stunningly amazing things, and I wonder if she somehow kick-started some of those dead functions to be less...dead when she was in control."

It made sense and seemed completely impossible at the same time. Then again, that was apparently turning into the story of my life.

As D and I walked back up the stairs, my hand in his, I looked up at him. "I'm going to have to see a psychiatrist now," I said quietly. "I...can't stay like this. I can't be a mother like this, you know? If we're going to have a baby, and the gods be willing, we will see it through and have our child, I... can't be like this."

He stopped on the stairs just shy of the top and turned to look down at me. "I'll support whatever you decide," he said quietly. "I just want you to be healthy and happy."

"Then I need to do this," I said, feeling the frustrating choking of tears that would never come clogging my throat. Couldn't Anne do something about that?

"Then I'll be here with you the whole time," he said, bending down to kiss me.

I felt like maybe I did have a chance to be okay after all.

☾○☽

So, there you have it. I'm a woman's body with the minds of five, including a child and a man. Want to talk about your chaos?

I'm in therapy now. My therapist encouraged me to write this. It started as journals, which each alter (as they are called) could use to track things and communicate. That's how Eve agreed to help me. This story could not have been told without the perspectives of more than just me, seeing as how so much of it ended up being lost on me.

This felt almost more like Eve's story than mine, but then, she is me. I am her. I am them.

Some of you will call me a liar. You'll say that I'm crazy, but not in that way. You aren't in my head and you haven't lived my life, so please don't assume. I've told you the truth of what I am and the story of how I finally learned it all.

My therapist is helping me 'integrate' my different selves, though it's a very slow process, and we've decided to not try to integrate Anne until after the baby comes. That's still progressing fine, by the way. But if her denial is what got me pregnant and is keeping me so, I'll keep her until it's safe. Besides, integration is such a long process...

I'm tired now. This took a lot out of me, and now I worry

about what you all will think of me. But I cannot be anything other than truthful. There have been too many secrets, and that has to stop now.

This is my life. I have to live it now.

Thank you for reading.

PERSONAL RESPONSIBILITY

I sat in the chair on the other side of my boss's desk, watching her read over the report I had just placed in front of her. Crossing my legs, I leaned back in my seat and crossed my arms over my chest to keep from chewing my already-devastated fingernails. I could see her eyebrows keep lifting like she wanted to look at me but was stopping herself, and my foot started swinging in the air entirely of its own accord.

"Torres," she finally said, closing the folder and setting it just to her left. She said my name but then nothing else, just took a deep breath and rested her elbows on the desk. She folded her hands, leaning her chin against them. I was just about to tell her that she had in fact gotten my name right, anything to prompt her, when she continued. "I can't do anything."

"Oh, come on," I all but whined. Uncrossing my legs, I planted my feet on the FBI regulation carpet and leaned toward her. "Nobody died." It seemed I put more weight on the zero-count death tally than anyone else.

"You discharged your preternatural abilities on a suspect," she stated, sounding exasperated.

I held up my hands with a shrug. "I didn't shoot anyone!"

She didn't look impressed. "Frankly, it would have been less paperwork for me if you had. Do you know the current agency regulations and filing for a DPA?"

DPA equaled Discharge of Preternatural Abilities. It was a brave (insane) new world.

My name is Serafina Torres, and I'm an agent with the Federal Bureau of Investigations, stationed in the preternatural satellite office in Boston, Massachusetts. In the years since Cameron's Law, making all preternatural beings legal citizens of the United States, the country had changed—had to change—a great deal. Now there were things like the preternatural satellite office of the FBI. As an electrokinetic—which meant I could create and/or control electrical currents—I was assigned there.

Basically, I'm a human taser.

In the case before us, that was all I did. I used my abilities to stop a suspect who was running. He didn't die, although he did end up in the hospital for a few days. Just like when any force is exercised on a suspect, you file a report. I was sitting in front of my boss, hoping that there wouldn't be too much trouble rolling down the mountain about it. I didn't feel like riding a desk.

I didn't reply to her question, because I didn't think anything that would come out of my mouth would actually help. She sighed, either frustrated with me or relieved that I didn't speak.

"You're not going to be shelved," she assured me, and I blew out a breath. "However, you're not going to like what you'll do instead."

"I hate it when you do that." I narrowed my eyes at her and waited.

"Protective detail."

"Babysitting?!" I sounded like a teenager asked to babysit their toddler sibling, but I didn't bother trying to correct myself. I'd been working under this woman for long enough that she knew me for who I was.

She looked thoroughly unimpressed with my annoyance. That was how it usually was, so I wasn't bothered. I knew that nothing I said could change her mind.

Dropping my head, I sighed.

"Who?" I asked, defeated.

I saw the edge of a file folder enter my vision. Without looking at her, I took it and opened it. Inside, there was a picture clipped to the top left. The name was Ben Collins, and from a quick look at the image, I would guess he had some Pacific Islands in there. Maybe he was from Hawaii. Although why anyone would leave islands like that to come to chilly New England, I couldn't guess. Reviewing the stats, I saw that he was a vampire, but a young one. It had only been a few years since he turned.

"He's a witness for the murder trial of Cameron St John," my boss said before I got to that part. That automatically made my eyes widen as I looked up.

It was widespread knowledge by now that a top-level member of LOHAV—the League of Humans Against Vampires—had been arrested for the murder of Cameron St John, the werewolf who introduced the Preternatural Rights Act in the first place, back in 2010. He and his girlfriend Sadie Stanton had been attacked. Cameron was killed, and Sadie nearly.

But it had been years, and there had never been enough information to make an arrest. I now knew what had changed, but they'd been keeping word of a witness pretty tightly locked.

"As you can imagine," she continued, "we are highly concerned for his safety. Members of the LOHAV organization have been known to attack and kill preternatural citizens on the street for less reason than being a star witness for the prosecution of one of their elite."

Suddenly, this job looked much bigger.

"So far, we have no reason to believe that his identity has been leaked; we don't even think his existence has been leaked, but we're taking no chances. He's a vampire and completely vulnerable in daylight, so a guard during those hours is going to be the most important. I plan to have an agent on him at all times. We have to swap out the daytime agent, and you'll be taking his place. Only one more week until he testifies."

"So you're not really punishing me for the DPA?" I asked with a small half-smile.

"Not really," she agreed with a mirror expression. "Still, this will get you out of everyone's line of sight for a while."

I nodded. "When do I start?"

☾O☽

It took a whopping two whole days before my 'quiet' daylight assignment went from standard to 'shit got real.'

Contrary to popular belief, vampires don't sleep in coffins in mansions better suited to Miss Havishim. Ben Collins lived in a modest first-floor apartment, with one bedroom sealed off with heavy, oversized blackout curtains. As a young vamp, he was going down halfway through dawn and not waking until full dark. The night agent showed up before that happened and I arrived after dawn, so I never even spoke to him. He kept to his dark room in that coma vamps go to during daylight hours. I played on my laptop, caught up on paperwork, and started reading a new book.

This all changed on my third day.

It started with the smell of something burning. Instinct made me jump up and rush to the oven in his small, stuffed-in-a-corner kitchen. I happen to hold the world record for burned cookies and muffins, so the smell of burning anything made me jump and think I'd done it again. It took until I had a grip on the oven door's handle before I remembered that I wasn't cooking anything.

That's when the smoke detectors went off.

My human brain just shrieked: fire, panic! My FBI brain told me that someone had found out about our witness and where he lived. They were going to burn him alive while he was temporarily dead to the world. It might not have been the case, but I suspected. Whatever the source of the fire, however, one thing was before me: I had to get Collins out.

During daylight hours, vampires are asleep. It's a coma-like state that no amount of effort can wake them from. Only the sun can do that, and only by setting. Otherwise, the sun isn't exactly healthy for them. A little can burn; a lot can destroy.

It didn't pass my notice that this could be a ploy to get Collins out of the building; him like a dead man, and me compromised by dealing with his body. I checked the door and found the hall clear and traces of fire licking the end of it through the open door of another apartment. I rushed in and called for backup and emergency services as I ran to the bedroom. The space was so short that I had only just gotten a person on the line as I opened the door.

I was explaining the situation very hurriedly as I looked into the pitch-black room. Even though I couldn't afford the time, I was momentarily disoriented. In the age of electronics, and my chronic curtain shortfall, I had never seen a truly dark room. Only the light from the open door I stood in fell on anything, but it was enough to guide me to his body.

I almost tried to wake him, just out of habit, but caught myself. I finished with the phone and stuffed it into my pocket as I hurried to the side he laid on.

By quick estimation, I guessed Collins was 5'9" or thereabouts and happily not a big man. However, I'm only 5'5" and unlike shifters in human form, human psychics don't have super strength. At least I kept up with my physical fitness as a fed. I knelt and pulled his dead weight to the edge of the bed and over my shoulders in a sort of firemen's carry. Grunting with the effort, I stood and staggered awkwardly out of the room. Both the smell of smoke and the smoke itself was getting stronger.

Not bothering to hide my noises of exertion, I made my way across the small apartment and to the door. I fumbled to get it open, finding the handle was already growing hot. I knew that was a bad sign. Entering the hallway, panicked people ran past me to get to the door. I followed a half-clad man down the smoky passage and to the exit.

Sunlight poured through the door as a stark reminder of the guy on my back and what his species was. I held him with one arm as I struggled to pull my gun, just in case this was a trap.

As I emerged, I didn't see any obvious threats. The overhang above the door kept the sun off us for the moment, but I could feel the heat behind me. Sirens were in the distance, but I had the bigger issue of the vampire now. He grew heavier by the moment, and I needed to put him *somewhere*.

I looked up and down the street, and my eyes fell on my car. I was parked at the curb not very far away.

Unfortunately, I had to holster my gun to get my keys. I staggered along the sidewalk and was more aware of the sun than I had ever been in my life. All I needed was to get my thumb on my key fob. I unlocked the doors twice, locked them, and set off the alarm as I jammed blindly at buttons before finally popping the trunk. I thought I heard sizzling behind me, but I couldn't be sure if I was imagining it as I threw him—not very gently, really—into my trunk. I slammed the door, cutting off all light and providing some safety as I turned back to the building.

Above all the noise, I heard someone calling for help. With my eyes already on the building, I saw someone carrying a child out. I guessed the little one couldn't be more than two and the woman was wailing. "My father is still in there! He can't walk very well, and I couldn't get them both!"

She sobbed around the words.

Again, my brain wondered if this was a trap...but could I live with myself if it wasn't?

"What apartment?" I demanded of her.

She had that panicked deer look for a moment, like she couldn't get past the screaming of her child and the smell of the smoke to comprehend my words. I shook her and asked again before she stammered the number.

Still on the first floor.

I ran into the building.

The smoke was clogging the hall now, and the heat hurt like hell. I crouched low and covered my mouth with my sleeve as I hurried forward, looking at door numbers.

1D. I hurried in and through the haze, I could see an elderly man with an obviously stiff leg trying to walk with his hands on the walls. I ducked under one of his arms. "Come on, sir," I said. "I'm a cop."

"Did Lisa get out?" He coughed before he finished the question.

"Yes," I replied, walking forward as quickly as the scenario would allow. "She and the kid are outside."

"Thank God." He sounded like he was crying, and I couldn't help feeling choked up. It was just the smoke, of course.

It was sensory overload and deprivation at once. I can't really recount how I made it out, but we did. Falling to the cement, I kind of dropped the guy but hey, we were out of the burning building. I hacked up a lung but managed to look up and see that my car was still there and with no signs of an open trunk.

If this had been a trick, it was the most detailed and yet least successful.

Leaving the woman, Lisa, to her father and child, I

pushed myself weakly to my feet and hurried to my car. I opened the trunk long enough to assure myself that the origami vampire was still there. He was, so I slammed the top shut and then sagged back to just breathe. My eyes stung, so I didn't bother looking at the source of the sirens drawing nearer.

❰O❱

A pair of agents came to take Collins—and my car with him— away to another, safer location. Meanwhile, I was down the street, sitting on the back of an open ambulance being offered oxygen that I swatted away, though I accepted the blanket because by now—with the adrenaline waning and fire further away—I was beginning to feel the late-winter chill, even if it was abnormally warm for late February. I watched my boss walk up.

"Are you okay, Torres?" she asked, folding her arms across her chest and eyeing me up and down like she could see the state of my lungs with just her eyes.

"Yes, sir," I replied simply. "Have they put the fire out?"

She nodded. "For the most part." Pausing, she glanced back at the building beyond the line of fire trucks. "They can't get in to investigate yet, but I'll bet anything that it was arson."

I sighed and resisted the urge to cough. "I would agree."

Her x-ray eyes returned to me. "Go home and get some rest," she said, turning and starting to walk away. She paused and looked back over her shoulder. "Good work, Torres."

"All I have to do to get a compliment is nearly burn to death," I said to myself and started chuckling, which made me start coughing, and the medic gave me the oxygen mask again.

☾○☽

My 'go home and rest' only lasted a few hours.

I got a call, which told me to wait for a car. The car came and took me to some nondescript building that I could barely make out in the dark. The agent who drove me, who I didn't know very well and didn't bother to try and fix that, walked me up to the door.

At the door, after some hoodoo I wasn't witness to, it opened to reveal my boss. She led me inside while the other agent left.

"He's asked to see you personally," she told me by way of greeting. And there was only one "he" this could be, given the day and the setting.

Ben Collins looked *almost* exactly like his picture. With a human, that would of course be expected. Vampires, however, don't change physically. I knew the image in his file had been after he was turned, so seeing that he had a scar at his hairline—pronounced with a small stripe of missing hair going back a couple of inches—was a surprise.

He stood up from the couch as I walked in, smiling as he held his hand out. I took it and shook.

"I am told that I have you to thank for the continuation of my un-life," he said with humor. "I never imagined I'd be so grateful for the trunk of a car."

His humor surprised me, and I laughed. "Yes, well. We work with what we have. I'm just glad it worked."

Collins inclined his head to me. "As am I, I assure you."

"Mr. Collins has asked that you be shifted to head up his protective detail from now on," my boss said. "That would put you on the night shift, starting tonight."

"If you're up to it, of course," he interjected. "I know that you took in some of that smoke."

Even if I hadn't been up to it, I never would have told them that. First off, because I didn't like admitting any kind of weakness in front of anyone. Secondly, this was a boon to my career, leading a detail and at the request of a star witness. I wasn't stupid enough to turn that down. I nodded instead. "I'm fine," I assured them.

"Good." My boss patted me on the shoulder and left.

"Well," Collins began a moment after we heard the door shut. "At least you will only have to put up with me for three nights, and then I testify." He gestured to the couch and we sat. "I hope to be better company living than dead, so to speak."

"I'm sure you're fine." I didn't settle in too much. Although we were now in a 'safehouse,' I remained on edge. After what happened to the last place, who could blame me? I had never been on a protective detail like this before. What did one talk about?

The protracted, awkward silence proved I wasn't the only one. He got up and went to the other room, and I took out my phone.

And that was how the rest of the night went.

☾O☽

I wasn't looking forward to work the next night.

After an exhausting day and the night shift, I had gone home and collapsed. I slept straight through the day and woke up only once the alarm went off.

Although I was happy that I had gotten recognition, as with most things, it wasn't all it was cracked up to be. It had been boring. Now I got to do it for another two nights before making sure he made it into the courtroom for his star testimony. I would say for a man living under the shadow of assassination, he looked pretty collected.

I relieved the agent on shift after I arrived and proved I was who I said I was—a process that was far more complicated in an age of shapeshifters. I settled in for another boring night, but Collins had other plans.

"May I call you Serafina?" he asked as we sat on the couch. The television was on some reality show, but the sound was low.

"If you like," I said. "Friends call me Sera."

He smiled, resting his arm on the back of the couch. "I don't know I know you that well, but then again, you shoved me in a car trunk. That suggests we must be on friendly terms." He paused when I couldn't help but chuckle. "You're more than welcome to call me Ben."

It was hard to miss that he was, indeed, a good-looking man, but he also had a disarming way about him. I wasn't sure that was a good thing when you were required to be all FBI around a person, but still, it put me at ease that this night would be less boring than the one before.

"All right, Ben," I said, wondering if this was improper behavior. I didn't really need another mark against me with the DPA still over my head.

I'd read his deposition once I'd officially been made lead on the case. I knew that he'd been leaving a friend's home when he'd heard the commotion and seen the tail end of the beating that killed Cameron St John—humans with brass knuckles made out of silver. As preternatural beings, like vampires and werewolves, are allergic to silver, it can damage them bad enough that a human could beat them to death.

Which was what happened. Ben saw it and witnessed those who ran away. They'd shot him with a silver bullet when they saw him and before he could escape. He 'went to ground' right away, which (I had recently learned) was when a vampire could sink into the ground into a coma far deeper than what happened to them during the day. It allowed their body to heal better, like a vampire's medical coma.

That explained the scar.

We chatted on and off through the evening. Around midnight found him standing and looking at the window. The shades were down, for protective reasons, but he looked like he wanted to see outside. I didn't blame him.

"Do you know why I was there that night?" He didn't specify what night, because we both knew I knew.

"Your deposition says you were visiting a friend," I replied, curious where this was leading.

He turned to me with a rueful smile. "A suicidal friend. I was talking him off the ledge, so to speak. I was trying to save a life, and then what happens? I'm too late to save another and nearly lose my own."

That surprised me. I couldn't reply for a moment then asked, "Would you do it again?"

"What's that?" His expression was curious.

"If you knew what would happen, would you still help your friend?" It might have seemed like a stupid question to most, but there were too many people out there that might say they wouldn't if they knew they would nearly be killed.

"Of course," he replied without hesitation. "It's why I'm here. No one knew I existed except the killers, and they wouldn't tell anyone. When I finally healed enough to rise, there was a cop car right at the end of the street. I went straight for him to tell him what'd happened and find out how long it had been. I didn't know until I rose."

He had the bullet. His blood and brain tissue was still on it, proving it was in his head, and the rifling matched a gun that had been registered to the defendant. It explained why they didn't shoot Cameron, but why had she brought it at all was the question. At the time, she had been a lowly member of the burgeoning LOHAV group but had risen quickly during the years to follow.

"Don't you believe that if you can act, you have a responsibility to do so?" he asked. "You joined the FBI, so you must feel some sense of responsibility for others."

"You've got me there," I said with a smile. "I was a cop first."

"Why did you join the force?" He returned to the sofa and sat down, turning his body to face me.

I narrowed my eyes at him, but not with actual rancor. "I'm the cop. Aren't I supposed to be asking the questions?"

He smiled. It was full of teeth, but his fangs were 'at rest.' He said nothing, but the expression was just as disarming.

"I guess it's what you said, I felt a responsibility. There's shit everywhere, bad things happening to people. I guess I thought I could…do something. And my grades weren't good enough to be a doctor." I chuckled, shaking my head. "I guess that doesn't make me particularly unique. Shouldn't I be telling some dramatic story about what led me to this job?"

"Life isn't always dramatic."

My brows lifted. "Says the vampire star witness against the nation's biggest anti-preternatural organization?"

That made him laugh. "Well, my life wasn't so dramatic before that."

"You were turned into a vampire," I pointed out. "Wasn't that dramatic?"

"Remarkably? Not really. It wasn't violent or a surprise. It was a mutual agreement." He shrugged casually, leaning into the back of the couch and resting his head on the fist.

I smiled. "I guess that makes us a couple of boring people."

☾O☽

The next night saw us playing poker. Never play poker with

a vampire.

He had just raised the bet when there was a knock at the door. We both tensed, and I pulled my gun, starting for it. Someone called the password, though, and I relaxed. I didn't put my gun away however, not until I was absolutely sure.

I kept the burglar chain on as I opened the door to check through it.

I was greeted with the business end of a can of mace straight to the eyes. I shrieked and stumbled back a step. "Saferoom!" I shouted, pawing at my eyes as I heard someone start banging against the door to break the chain. I kept my gun tight but down while I couldn't see and instead lifted my free hand, loosing a random shot of my electrokinesis. Someone let out a strangled sound.

Forcing my eyes open, I could see blurry images. Someone was on the ground in front of the door, but I thought I saw a second. I released another stream, but they dodged back. I stepped back and dug my phone out of my pocket, calling the office for help. There was supposed to be an agent outside the building as well. What had happened to him?

As I staggered past the table where the poker chips and deck of cards remained, I saw that Ben wasn't there so he must have taken my command.

My vision was slowly coming back as I hurried to find him, who was in the small room hidden off the closet. I entered and nearly got my throat torn out before he recognized me. I stared at him in the dim light for a moment.

"I wonder why you need protection," I whispered, gesturing for him to follow me.

This hidden room connected to stairwell that led to the basement and then an exit. It was an old building with many odd quirks, which made it ideal as a safehouse. I could feel my magic lingering just under my skin, unlike the pits of my mind where I usually stuffed it. It was like static electricity to normal people, that feeling that no matter what you do, you'll spark when you touch something.

I kept my gun out and held up, even if holding it and my magic so close together was painful.

This stairwell was narrow and dark. I knew he could see in the dark, but I wasn't feeling so great about it. However, knowing it was a straight shot, I knew I wouldn't get lost. I was more worried about someone following, but so far so good.

We reached the basement, and some moonlight came through the high windows. I scouted everything and then went to the door. It was a non-descript wood creation at the very back of the building, overlooked by most unless they were looking for it. I checked to make sure that Ben was still with me and then I opened the door, using my aching eyes to peer out.

I saw a muzzle flash in the darkness and just barely slammed the door before a bullet drove itself into the door frame. My heart tried to crawl out of my mouth but instead a stream of curses that would make a sailor brush came free.

Right as they started banging on the door there, I heard them back at the metal door that led from the stairwell.

"Get down!" I shouted and dropped my gun, putting my hands out to either side—one toward the wooden door and one toward the metal. I rarely had reason to stretch my powers this much, but desperate times... Electricity shot like lightning from both hands, striking bolts into the cement of one side and the metal frame of the other.

The result was a blocked wooden door and a melted metal frame.

I passed out.

☾O☽

When I woke, it took me a moment to remember where I was...and then I sat up like a shot. It was so fast that my head immediately swam and I fell back, only to realize that my head had been on his legs. Blinking up at him, I sat up again—this time more slowly—and looked around. We were still in the basement, and the doors were still blocked.

"You weren't out for long," he answered the question I hadn't asked. "If they're still trying to get in, it's been quietly. I haven't heard anything for a while now."

I rubbed my eyes, which still hurt, and then dug my phone out of my pocket. I realized it hadn't broken when I fell. Unfortunately, there was no signal down here either. I knew I had gotten my call out, but where were they?

"I can't tell if this means I'm good at my job or really bad," I quipped with a half-smirk, rubbing my neck. I looked around at the small basement. There were two windows, less than twelve inches high, toward the very top. I wondered why they hadn't tried breaking them in, but then I remembered how many plants were growing around the foundation. Maybe they couldn't see them.

"I'm not dead," he replied. "Or at least not in a more permanent state of death. That's something."

I chuckled. It was something.

☾○☽

I heard the sirens about fifteen minutes later, right about the time I began doubting I'd actually talked to anyone in the first place. I heard some shouting, then someone tried to open the door, and then someone banged on the windows. I grabbed my gun, just in case, but heard my boss's voice shouting through a few minutes later and let out a breath of relief.

"How well can a vampire move a pile of fractured cement?" I asked him with a tired smirk.

☾○☽

Despite their best attempts, Ben Collins made it to court and gave his testimony. The defense attorney tried to trip him up, but they really do give you a Cool, Calm, and Collected spell when you become a vampire. He tripped over nothing and just glided through, totally together. I still didn't know him that well, but I couldn't help but feel a little proud.

Ben would remain under guard until the trial ended, but we were betting that LOHAV wouldn't try as hard now that he had testified. Revenge was an issue, but a little less of one. We moved him to a new safehouse, and there was an investigation—separate to my protective detail—to find out how they'd learned the two addresses. We suspected a leak, but that was my boss's problem...until they showed up at our door again.

While Ben sat at the corner of the couch reading a book, I sat at the small dining table with my boss.

"So, do I get that DPA wiped off my record for a job well done?" I asked with a half-smile as I nodded back at Ben. I glanced over and saw him lift his eyes, smiling over the edge of the open novel.

"Yes," my boss replied, to my surprise. "Only to add two more."

"Oh, come on!" I exclaimed. She gave me The Look. I sighed and then smiled weakly. "At least I didn't shoot anyone?"

WOLF'S BANE

Three.

Whether a number had meaning wasn't really something I used to give a lot of thought to. Numerology was never my thing, so aside from math classes that I never enjoyed, even if I got good grades, I never thought about numbers much. I had no idea just how significant the number three would become for me, or how like the Hester's scarlet A, it would start meaning one thing and come to mean something very different. It would go from something not good to something surprising.

February 29th

The night had been appropriately cold when we walked into the courtroom. By the time the verdict was read, I felt that cold inside me.

I thought I would have felt different than that, but I just felt cold.

My name is Madison St John. I was in a Suffolk County Superior Court courtroom in Boston that night because after eight days and my certainty we were looking at a hung jury, the verdict in the case of the Commonwealth of Massachusetts versus Sally Barton was to be announced.

"Guilty on the charge of murder in the first degree. Guilty on the charge of conspiracy to commit murder in the first degree. Guilty on the charge of attempted murder in the second degree."

A collective gasp of shock moved through the people, although everyone was divided about the nature of their shock. Most of the preternatural beings had been sure it would be either not guilty or a hung jury. It would only take one bigot to cause a mistrial, but that wasn't the case. Justice had actually won out. As such, I was sure that the rest of the gasps were of disgust from the anti-preternatural group in attendance.

I knew that the next few weeks were going to be filled with vitriol flung at us like shit from monkeys, but it wasn't anything we hadn't weathered before.

Sadie and I exchanged a look that said everything without words. After all these years, we didn't think there would ever be justice for my brother. He had been murdered like a dog in the streets, and Sadie nearly taken with him, for the simple reason that he was a werewolf and thought he should be allowed to say so.

Tears pricked at my eyes and I sniffled, wiping the corners. Chance's big arm wrapped around my shoulders and pulled me into his side. I pressed my cheek to his jacket and closed my eyes, gathering my center again.

Slowly, the crowd began to file out. The four of us—Sadie and Vance, me and Chance—waited until most of the gallery had already left. When I looked up, I saw Ben Collins. He had been the star witness, at great personal risk to himself. I couldn't help but walk over to him. It was the first chance I'd had to speak with him. There was a woman beside him. I smelled cop.

"Mr. Collins," I said, holding out my hand with a sincere smile. "I can't thank you enough, sir."

He took my hand but held my gaze for a moment, curious before he put the pieces together and nodded. "Ms. St John," he said, returning my smile but in an otherwise respectful, sober expression. "It was the right thing to do."

The woman beside him smiled slightly. "We all have a responsibility to do the right thing when it's put before us, right?"

Turning to her for a moment, he smiled and nodded. "We do," he agreed and then back to me. "I'm just glad that justice was served. It was about time."

"Yes," I agreed. "Yes, it was." Before I started crying again, I bid them farewell and returned to the others. Chance wrapped his long fingers around my hand, and we fell in step behind Sadie and Vance as we made our way out of the courtroom. Our little group was quiet as we moved through the hallway, although not everyone shared our sobriety.

"*Monsters!*" a woman screamed. She was standing beside the wall and recognized us instantly. None of us were without notoriety. As Cameron's girlfriend when he began the legislation for legality, Sadie was a poster girl for preternatural rights. I was there with them as his sister. Vance had been in the papers for his high-profile cases, and Chance was a well-known heavyweight in boxing's preternatural division. Just the sight of us was enough to pin us for the not-human beings we were.

I stopped and looked at her. I hoped she would change her mind, but I knew she wouldn't.

"You are abominations!" she continued, coming toward us and waving a pointed finger. "You should all be sent back to the holes you crawled out of! When this world comes to its senses, that law and everyone like it will be taken back and then you'll be hunted down like the monsters you are!"

Chance's body went rigid with tension beside me. Vance radiated it so much that I didn't need to be touching him to know. "Chance," I warned in a low voice. My boy had a temper and often wrestled with self-control, I knew this. I knew just as well that you never engaged with the bigots. Don't get into a fight with an idiot or they'll drag you down to their level and beat you with experience.

I could hear Sadie's low voice convincing Vance of the same wisdom. He'd had temper issues since being turned, but he'd had been doing better. I couldn't worry about him, however, since I had my own hothead to worry about.

Turning my body, I moved in front of him. At 5'6", I had to lean up on my toes to get as close to his 6'5" face as I could. I put my hands on his cheeks and forced his gaze down to mine, holding his fierce cat-eyed glare. "Chance," I said, low enough for his ears. "It's not worth it. Let her be, and we'll go on about our night."

It took several moments before his shoulders relaxed just enough to tell me that he had listened. After another moment, he nodded and let out a long breath. He cast a few more eye-daggers at the woman, but slid his arm around me and we all started walking back out.

☾O☽

The two-and-a-half-hour drive from Boston to Adelheid was pretty quiet. We let the radio play while Vance drove and Sadie was lost in thought. I sat in the middle of the backseat and leaned against Chance. I didn't sleep, but I did feel like I was dozing a little. Long drives could have that effect on a person, even a werewolf.

When we got back to the house, we all bid each other good night. Sadie and Vance went straight to their bedroom. Dawn was still a few hours away, but we all needed some quiet time.

"I should head out, babe," Chance said as we stood by the front door.

"Are you sure?" I asked. I had never given him grief about when he needed to leave, but that night, I was just feeling...needy. I bit my lip as I ran my hands along the lapels of his leather jacket. "Can't you just stay the rest of the night? I really could use you here."

He frowned slightly, debating my request and his schedule. It seemed that I won. He nodded and leaned down to kiss me. I smiled, grateful, and led the way to my bedroom.

All the clothes came off right away, but we didn't have sex or anything. The beasts inside of us shifters are like our animal versions, and we can be very tactile. Laying under the blankets of my full-size bed, which really wasn't big enough for him, I just desperately needed to feel his skin against mine. There was comfort in that, and I needed comforting.

He left shortly after dawn, and I forced myself to go back to sleep in my empty bed.

March 15th

Marriage really does change things, or maybe just our perception of things. I had never felt like the 'third wheel' around Sadie and Vance before, but living in the house with them since they had gotten married... Well, I'd started feeling increasingly uncomfortable. It wasn't that they did anything or treated me different. I just felt different.

We all had dinner together that night. Sadie and Vance both drank theirs, but they cooked for me. They were leaving on a business trip shortly thereafter, so we had the meal together before they left. It was pleasant, but again...third wheel. They did most of the talking, and then went to get their bags and head out.

However, as much as I felt like the wheel, I didn't like the empty house either.

Wolves are pack animals. We are social creatures. And humans, however hard they try to think they need to be independent, are tribal. So werewolves? Like to be around others. We like other werewolves the best but will take anyone we have a connection with. There is the occasional loner, but they are rare and even rarer still are those who *want* to be. So, I went out. I was due at Gabriel's shortly anyways, so it all worked out.

Feeling a little lonely, I called Chance in the car on the way. Technically against the law in this state, but so was the ten miles over the speed limit I habitually drove, so...

It didn't matter anyways, because it went straight to voicemail. I knew he was a pretty busy guy, so I left a quick message to say that nothing was wrong and hung up. I drove the rest of the way across town to the home of Gabriel Raines, the alpha of Adelheid's werewolf pack. It was one of the biggest in the region, accounting for several hundred members of the city's population. They did not all show up at all functions, thankfully, but they were still associated with the pack and different gatherings brought different members.

Like any organization, it required administration. Maybe it's funny to say that a werewolf pack did, but it did. Gabe was a great leader but a lousy secretary. Since he was without an alpha female, his wife having left him a couple years back, I had agreed to help out when I decided to officially join the pack a few months back. It was what I did for a living, after all.

I arrived. For a change, there weren't a bunch of other wolves at his house. While the pack didn't have a group living space like the coven did, it was still somewhat communal. Like all the kids hanging out at mom and dad's, even though they had their own places.

Parking in the driveway, I walked up and knocked. He let me in, and we walked into the office.

Gabriel Raines was a tall man. Not as tall as Chance, but close. He was handsome in an intense sort of way, and he could be a little too serious and a little too in charge, in that way that alphas could be, but he was a good man. He cared a great deal about his pack and took care of us. I couldn't figure out why he hadn't remarried, or even found a long-term relationship, but it wasn't something I asked about.

Although, his personal life was kind of in front of everyone now.

"Ready for the full moon fight?" I asked, teasing a little, as I sat down at the computer.

"How is anyone ever ready for that?" he replied with a rueful smile. His hazel eyes flickered as he sat beside me.

I was about to open the website for the pack's mailing list—several hundred people can be hard to keep in touch with—but had to turn to face him. I laughed, almost embarrassed that I couldn't help myself. "How can you do this?"

He smiled again and knew exactly what I meant. "Why not?" he asked, shrugging his broad shoulders. "I'm obviously not having any luck picking a mate, so maybe our ancestors didn't have a bad idea. The pack needs two alphas."

Our lycanthrope roots trace our traditions back to the merging of man and beast. Our rituals do not resemble how our 'real' animal counterparts behave in nature but as a combination and interpretation that has progressed through the ages. It works for us.

Ascension to leadership as alpha male happens by way of a fight between all the eligible male wolves in the pack, and any from outside who want a shot. The strongest and the cleverest, the one who balances the wolf and the man, comes out on top and leads from then on. At least, until he retires or dies, or unless he's challenged and defeated. The latter is rare. Usually, a pack alpha is forced by human reasoning to resign.

In the days of our ancestors, there would then be an alpha female fight. That winner would become pack alpha female and marry the alpha male, then they would lead together. Now, the female fight was stopped long ago. The alpha male would pick his own mate to help him lead, but Gabriel hadn't found anyone.

When the pack elders suggested the old ways, he had agreed.

"You're a braver man than I, Gabriel," I said with a grin that showed I realized I wasn't a man in the first place.

I turned to the computer as he chuckled. "Alright, so, reminder for the fight," I said, opening up a browser and then the newsletter site. I went through the process and typed in information. As I did so, my brain started looking at things from a more professional viewpoint. Something occurred to me that made me stop and turn toward him again. "Have you thought about security?"

He met my gaze, and his dark brows drew down slightly. "We'll have the enforcers," he said, sounding uncertain about what I was asking.

"Several of whom are female and likely in the fight," I pointed out. "The agency has been getting piles of hate mail since the verdict. I mean, literal *piles* of illiterate, xenophobic bullshit, practically back to the legality trial levels. I just started thinking about this huge group of us out in the middle of the woods at night... Maybe we should be concerned about having a little extra security."

"That's a good point," he said, sounding a little like he wished he'd thought of it himself. "Did you have something in mind?"

"Yeah, actually," I said with a half-smile. "Vampires."

"Vampires?" Now, he was really surprised.

I laughed, a little sheepishly. "Yeah. I mean, I know we all haven't always been the best of buddies, but we have a common cause in the safety of our species. And with Sadie and Vance and me, I think Jade and Shayna would agree to help. Jade knows how to be politic, and it would be a smart move for her. I'm sure if I asked nicely, she would."

He smiled at me like he was thinking something I couldn't guess. "You'd be willing to talk to her for me?"

"Sure, I know her a bit by now," I replied easily.

"That would be great, thanks." He nodded. That intense gaze settled on me, and I almost began to feel a little uncomfortable. A look like that felt like it could penetrate a person's soul, and I wasn't sure I wanted anyone looking that deep. "Hey, I don't suppose you've considered joining into the fight yourself, have you?" He paused and rubbed the back of his neck. "You'd be great as alpha. You're smart, you think of the pack, you're good at all the stuff I'm not, you and I get along really well, you're gorgeous…" He trailed off.

Before I could properly reply, he surprised me again. I managed to take a breath and open my mouth, but lips were made busy and breath was taken when he kissed me on very obvious sudden impulse.

I couldn't help myself, but I kissed him back. His lips were so warm, and werewolves can sense each other better than any other creatures we encounter. I liked him, a lot. It was hard not to be drawn to a good man with a good heart, and of course, the commanding alpha nature without verging into total asshole helped a lot. Leaning forward, I kissed him back, and it felt good…

…up until the moment it felt wrong.

I thought of Chance. I knew this wasn't precisely against the rules, but even if we said we could, I hadn't really dated anyone else. I guess it made it kind of easy against the random tide of dating that could happen to have this boyfriend just out there. This was the first time I was truly tempted, and maybe if circumstances had been different…

"I can't join the fight," I said, sounding breathless even to my own ears. "I have a boyfriend…"

"I thought that was all pretty casual?" Gabe asked.

"Yes." I laughed softly, realizing that even though we'd stopped kissing, we hadn't really moved very far apart. "It is, but I think marriage would be a pretty big issue if I won. And if I didn't, you'll be marrying someone else."

He took a deep breath, nodded, and leaned back. He ran both of his hands through his hair, pushing it off his face. "Good point," he said ruefully. "Your reasonableness just makes me wish more that you were joining the fight, but I do understand."

I smiled, although I knew I forced it. I was painfully tempted to kiss him again, but I stopped myself. We got back to work, because that was why I had been there in the first place. It was much harder to focus after that. I became more aware of his masculine presence than I had been before, but I used will power I didn't know I had to ignore it until I was done.

We bid farewell pleasantly and I left.

Once in the car, I called Chance again while still sitting in Gabe's driveway. Voicemail. So, trying to move past that, I called Jade. As I had predicted, she saw the wisdom in the idea and agreed to send Shayna and some of her wardens to help. I thanked her profusely and then went to work.

☾ ◯ ☽

Work when Sadie was around was very different than work when she wasn't. When she was gone, I was in charge. Truth was that while I didn't want Sadie to go anywhere, ever, I did kind of like being in charge. That night, the feeling made me think a lot about what Gabriel had said about being a good alpha. I realized that, situation being different, I probably would have joined the fight.

I thought I could be a good alpha. I could lead, and I wanted to help take care of my pack, and being married to

Gabriel didn't sound like the worst thing in the world…but the idea of giving up Chance to do it, I didn't think I could. I loved him. But I also knew that our relationship wasn't ever going to be more than it was.

The night came and went. I only had to break up Dakota and Edward once. The only demon to get free was a little one, and that was an improvement. (A demon got loose at least once every two or three nights, but compared to other summoners and his exceptional summing skills? Donovan's record was fantastic.)

I shut down the office about an hour before dawn. That was pretty standard operating for a preternatural-oriented business. The timeframe shifted with the seasons, of course. Having a vampire for a boss kind of had a big effect on that. The daytime secretary would come in a couple of hours later. He was basically a glorified answering machine who would take over for the not-glorified one. We didn't get as many calls during the day as at night, but he helped with some of the filing and so forth too.

When I got back to the house, it was…still empty. I knew it would be, but knowing a thing and unlocking your door to it were two different things.

I sulked my way to the kitchen, because in that situation, it served as a movement verb. I got something to eat and went straight to my room, eating in bed after getting changed. I was done and settling under the covers with the television on—legalization had made overnight programming much better—when my phone beeped. I had gotten a text message, which I took a look at. It was from Chance: *hey baby sry missed ur call. busy. will call u ltr.*

With a sigh, I put my phone back on the table and fell asleep with a late-night crime drama playing. I dreamed of Chance and Gabe. Of cats and dogs.

March 16th

It was afternoon when I woke up. Everything felt dry, and my face felt tight. I wondered if I'd been crying in my sleep, which would have been weird. I was slow to actually get out of bed, but I managed to. I turned on the television sets in my room and the living room, putting them on loud so the house didn't sound empty while I did laundry and cleaned the kitchen.

I thought about Sadie and Vance, being married. I thought about D and Cassandra, having their miracle baby. Even Dakota, miss grumpy herself, was in a settled relationship. And there I was, feeling ready to move into a more serious phase of my life and in love with a man who would never move into that phase himself. We'd talked about it, and I'd always said it was cool.

Now, I was starting to realize that maybe I wasn't as cool with it as I thought.

By evening, I called the office. Lorelei (Edward's fiancée) was manning the phones for me because it was the full moon. Legally, all shifters had to get the full moon off if they worked a night job, and most did. We didn't necessarily have to get paid, but we couldn't get penalized for it. Of course, having the boss as my almost-sister helped that. Being the one who handled payroll didn't hurt either.

Lorelei usually wasn't in the office, busy with her dog rescue, but since Sadie wasn't there either, we were a little short-staffed…because *no one* wanted Dakota on the phones.

At dusk, I finally changed out of my pajama pants and T-shirt into clothes for the night. After that, I called Sadie because I knew she'd be up. She didn't precisely sound awake when she answered the phone, but she wasn't in a coma, so I was good.

"I have a problem," I said, sitting on the edge of my bed

as I pulled on my shoes. I knew I wouldn't be wearing them for long.

"Good evening to you too," Sadie replied. "What's going on? Is it something at the office?"

I let out a huffy breath. "No, it's *my* problem." I laid it all out pretty quick. She knew about the alpha female fight already, but I told her about the conversation with Gabe the night before, and all of the thoughts that I had been having about him, the pack, and Chance.

When I was done, she was quiet for a moment. "I can't tell you what to do, Madison," she finally said. "I want you to be happy. I guess as clichéd as it might be, you have to just... follow your heart."

It was convenient that I needed to pull the phone away to put on my jacket—it was March, after all—so I was able to look at the phone in irritation. "Really? I could have read that on a fortune cookie, Sadie. I'm looking for serious advice here."

I heard her laugh and then water running. "That *is* serious advice," she replied. "Did you think I could tell you what you should do?"

That made me wilt. "I guess? You have before."

Her sympathetic expression was audible. "That was about taking a vacation. This is your whole life, so I can't, and you know that. I guess you have two choices. You love Chance and when you see him, he makes you happy. But that's when he's around, and it's not often. Does he fulfill you? You don't love Gabe, but you could. You would have stability and other things that you want out of life. So, you have to decide which is the most important to you."

That put it all out pretty starkly. It didn't help me choose, but it drew the lines.

I got into the car and started it up. "Thanks, Sadie." I pulled out onto the road and headed toward the largest tract of forest in the city. It was where the pack always met for our full moon runs, having a convenient clearing right in the center for us to gather and then all those trees for a big group of wolves to run around in.

Werecreatures can change whenever they want, but at the time of the full moon, we *have* to. The moon will compel us even if we resist. Being social creatures, the werewolves always make an event out of it and gather to change together.

I pulled in behind a long line of cars of all shapes, sizes, and ages. The cars themselves were a pretty good representation of just how different the pack was. The only thing some of us had in common was being a werewolf, but for this night at least, we were family.

Parking and locking my doors, I joined the stream of people trickling into the trees. We smiled and greeted one another, and I took a mental note of just how many I saw. It seemed that the female fight was drawing more than the usual crowd for a full moon run. I wondered how many of them might have shown up to join the fight, since I couldn't help but notice quite a few of them were women.

A strange twinge of...jealousy, perhaps, stung me.

Ignoring it, I moved to the designated 'spots.' We can't shift without either taking off or destroying our clothing, so for these nights, we have safe spots for said personal items. They would be guarded during the night. Since nudity isn't an issue for shifters, we all just stripped down and put away our belongings. Then we began the painful process of transforming. It only lasted about a minute but hurt like hell.

After we were changed, the enforcers changed as well. It was just safe practice to not have us all in the middle of the transformation at once, since it couldn't be stopped once started. It made us vulnerable.

As soon as I was a wolf, I could smell the vampires. They weren't easy to see, blending into the darkness, but a faint trace of the grave remained where they were. It wasn't something I could smell as a human—thankfully, given that I lived with two of them—but I could as a wolf. The smell was comforting to me right then, however, because it meant they had our backs.

Once all in our animal forms, we moved to the clearing. We lined it completely, multiple wolves deep. I held some respect for being Cameron's sister and got a spot up front. I took my place along the line and watched as, a few minutes later, it parted on the other side. I watched as maybe a dozen females walked, two by two, into the 'arena.' Gabriel came right behind them.

If he was handsome as a man, he was a sight to behold as a wolf. The largest of us all, with glossy, pure black fur. He walked like a creature in charge.

When he reached the center, six females went to each side and formed semi-circles. Gabriel stood there in the middle. After a moment of surveying the lot of us, he threw his head back and howled. We all threw our heads back and joined in, instinctively harmonizing to make twenty sound like fifty. Or a hundred sound like a thousand. It was music. And we all howled long and loud, and we were proud. We were not hiding ourselves, and the sweetness of that—even years later—had yet to go away.

Once he stopped, so did the rest of us. He moved back and took his place along the line, letting out one short bark to signal the fight.

The alpha male fight has always been a vicious thing to watch. The battle for dominance and the pure animal aggression... Well, watching the women fight was even more than that. Maybe a stereotype, not that I could call it a 'cat fight,' but it existed for a reason. Like liquor, the animal form takes down one's inhibitions. The human mind remains, but it is given free rein to some of its baser impulses.

I watched Marcia Windon leap on Stacy Kellar like the latter was nothing more than a field mouse. Being smaller, she yipped with pain almost immediately and rolled over in instant submission. She was allowed to leave the field without further harassment, while Marcia made a run for Wendy. I was relieved to see Stacy off the field. She was nineteen and put the word 'princess' to shame. She'd have made an awful alpha female.

Then again, as I surveyed the field—feeling the bloodlust and tension become contagious—I didn't think I liked any of the women for the role. I liked most of them personally but had trouble imagining myself being *led* by one.

Carmen had Henrietta at her throat relentlessly almost from the first moment and left the clearing shortly after Stacy. Everything moved so fast. The animal forms of shapeshifters are larger and faster and stronger than their in-nature equivalents. Three more were taken out and fast. Marcia was still in it, gunning for Henrietta next. Those two danced around one another, snarling and nipping. They traded bites rapidly, but neither stayed still long enough to get a grip for several minutes. In fact, two more were taken out while those two sparred.

Then I watched as Louise jumped on Marcia. Between the two, Marcia was forced into submission and departure.

That left four on the field.

I was watching the pair on one side and not paying nearly enough attention to the other. My body was rigid with adrenaline by this point, and the crowd almost vibrated with it. It was almost an audible sound that drew us all to those minute movements as if we were in the fight ourselves, even as we stood at the sidelines.

That second fight came barreling at me when I wasn't watching. Two rolled me. One remained unconscious while the other ran back to the arena, dragging me in. Pissed, I surged to my feet and lunged for the one who had run over me not once but twice. I jumped on her back, sending her crashing flat with a yelp. I smelled her blood and knew she was injured, the whimpering suggested my jumping on her made it worse. I nipped at her throat until she rolled over.

Grudgingly, I let her go and then felt someone hit me head-on in the side. I yelped in pain as I thought I felt something bruise, if not break. I crashed to my side but scrambled fast onto my feet. I would not let anyone keep me down! Whirling around, despite the pain, I turned on the one who had attacked me. She lunged and snapped, jumping back just as fast. I surged for her, snapping my teeth at air. She jumped forward, expecting me to jump back like she had, but I didn't. Instead, she jumped into my range while my teeth were still bared.

I slid to her side and snapped at her neck, grabbing her and shoving her to the ground. With a yip, she submitted and slunk away.

Growling, I whirled around until I realized…

…there wasn't anyone left.

The adrenaline bled out as I turned to look at Gabriel. His eyes were just as intense as a wolf as they were as a man, and that gaze burned into me now. I felt like he must have some kind of magic in the look, because my knees weakened.

Padding toward me slowly, he came within breathing range and then howled.

He howled. Everyone else howled. I didn't howl.

I remained in wolf form until everyone left. Then it was just Gabe and I standing in that clearing, which was when I had to shift back. He did as well. Once we were both human again, we stared at one another. He was even better looking without his clothing, I had to admit, but I wasn't thinking much about that. I was suddenly very confused.

I had convinced myself to sit it out. That made the choice easy, because someone else would win and it would be off the table. Now, though, it was right in front of me. There was no avoiding it.

"You don't have to agree, you know," Gabriel said first. He smiled sympathetically. "It won't be official until the equinox, so you have four days to say no. We'll do the fight again next full moon, and that will be that."

"I...am conflicted," I admitted with a weak smile. "I like you. I don't think being married to you would be so bad. I'd like to be alpha...but..."

"But...your kitty," he finished for me.

"Yeah," I admitted. My weretiger and our...whatever relationship. "I'll think about it. Okay?"

He held my cheek with his hand and leaned down, kissing me lightly. "You do that," he said, bowing his head slightly. "I would be honored to have you as my alpha and my wife, if you accept, but I will understand if you do not."

I sighed, feeling a little like I was melting—in the good and bad ways. "Why couldn't you be a jackass and make this easier?" I asked feebly.

Gabe just chuckled and turned away, going into the trees to put his clothing back on.

"Congratulations." A voice from behind me made me yip, sounding like a dog even in human form, and spin around. Shayna stood behind me with a smirk. "I don't know much about your procedures, but that seems like a suitable thing to say?"

"Yes," I agreed, putting my hand on my chest as my heart raced, from the fight, Gabe, and the startle. "Thank you. And thank you for being here. We appreciate you watching our backs and all that." I nodded at her. "If the wolves can help you all in the future, let us know."

Shayna nodded back. "We were glad to assist. Jade may be speaking with you about a daylight guard for the baby of D and Cassandra. Every moment passes and makes it more likely that it will be born. It will need someone to watch it while its parents are in the vampire coma, and the wolves seem the best to help. You have a large network, and humans would be too weak if there was trouble."

Despite my panic about my situation, mentioning The Baby made me smile. "I would be thrilled to organize assistance," I said sincerely.

She smiled again and made her farewells. In brief glimpses, I saw bodies I hadn't seen before fading into the forest, leaving me alone in the clearing with my thoughts, and a hard decision.

❰O❱

An emotional conversation while driving didn't really appeal to me, so I waited until I got home to call Chance. I just hoped that I didn't get his voicemail this time, because I really needed to talk to him. Luck was with me, or not depending on your point of view, and he answered for a change.

"Hey, babe," he said. "What's up?"

"Hi..." I began and then faltered. "Uh, there was the alpha female fight tonight." I swallowed hard. I usually didn't stumble this much, but this kind of thing wasn't something I was good at, and I didn't even know what I wanted to say. "I kinda accidentally won. I hadn't meant to join the fight because it means being alpha and marrying Gabe and I told him about you so I had meant to sit it out but then I got rammed into and the adrenaline was up and—" The words just poured out, and I couldn't stop them, until he interrupted me.

"Hey," he said. "Sugar, we always said this was casual. You got this thing and you gotta do it, so go do it. It's all good. Take care."

He hung up.

I sat with the phone to my ear, blinking at nothing. I had kind of expected him to say something like that, but not so abruptly. I thought maybe there would be some discussion, and that he'd let me say good-bye before he hung up.

Swallowing hard, I put my phone on my nightstand. I guess that made my decision for me, so why didn't I feel better about it?

March 17th

Sleep was miserable.

After getting home from the fight and then the conversation with Chance, if it could be called that, it took me hours to get to sleep. Dawn had happened before I achieved it, and it only lasted a few hours. It was filled with bad dreams that I could barely remember, along with a lot of tossing and turning.

The woman in the mirror had terrible bags under her eyes, and the blue was surrounded by bloodshot. I sighed. This was going to be a banner day, I could already tell. I brushed my teeth and put on a lot of makeup, hoping to cover it all. I really didn't want to look like an addict going through withdrawal.

Checking my phone, there were no calls or texts from Chance. Had I really expected there to be? I didn't know, but I was still disappointed. I did have a text from Gabriel: *I know you were upset last night, so I just wanted to make sure you were okay?*

That made me smile a little.

I didn't reply to it just yet and instead got myself into the car and to the supermarket. The house needed food, and I was the only one who'd stock it. Of course, I didn't have much of an appetite, but I knew that there were certain things I wanted to have in the house for when I stopped feeling like crap, so that was what I aimed for.

Of course, nothing was going quite how I planned it

lately.

At the store, I ran into Lisa Wilkes. She was a member of the pack, and I didn't really want to see any pack members just yet, but I didn't notice her until too late. There was no chance of hiding behind a display of soup cans, so I had to talk. Pleasantries passed quickly. I tried to make a break for it, but she pinned me.

"Could I talk to you for a moment?" she asked. The look in her eyes said this wouldn't be quick, but she started talking before I could run. "I'm worried about my son. Billy just seems, I don't know, so distant. I'm worried that he's going to go loner, and that's such a hard life. He grew up in the pack, I don't know if he would be able to make it. But he's so young, and he thinks he knows everything. I just don't want him to foolishly pick a bad path, you know?"

"I understand, Lisa," I said as sympathetically as my exhausted self could manage. "But nothing is official. I'm not your alpha, so I don't know if I'm the right person to ask advice."

"But you will be," she said quietly, and with such surety that it shocked me. Like she knew I'd say yes (of course, why would someone who had joined the fight say no) but also like she trusted me to be good at it. Like I was a person to look to for advice. It made me uncomfortable, but kind of in that good way. Like maybe this was the right course for me.

I managed a smile. "You can't dictate what your son does. He's still young, but he's pretty much legal by now. If you push too hard, he may pick a choice just to resist. Offer your advice, but give him room to make the choice. Being a loner is hard, but it isn't the end of the world, and it'll be easier to be without a pack than without a family because he felt pushed away."

Lisa looked a little crestfallen, like she'd hoped for something else, but then she smiled and picked up, nodding. "Yeah, yeah," she said. "I'll try to do that. It's hard, as a mother."

The smile grew a little as she patted my shoulder. Wolves are very tactile, so I didn't mind. "You'll understand when you have pups."

Children. I hadn't even thought of that, and the idea hit me with shock and terror and...excitement all at once. I had always wanted kids but had put the thought away for a while. But if I married Gabe and became alpha, well...

❮O❯

I went home long enough to put the groceries away. I took a shower, deciding that the people at the market could deal with me smelly but work shouldn't. After food, I headed to the office, but focusing was hard. I called Sadie to fill her in. She sounded very not surprised. I wasn't really sure what to make of that, but Sadie often knew me better than I knew me so I just accepted it.

Eight hours somehow dragged by and flew by at the same time. Nothing more from Chance, and just a couple quick texts with Gabe to assure him I was okay. I went home a few hours shy of dawn.

I had been home all of fifteen minutes, just long enough to change back into my pajama pants and t-shirt, when there was a knock at the door. Curiously, I went up to it and looked through the window. I relaxed when I saw Gabriel, moving to the door to let him in. Freshly washed, I could smell the soap, he came in and then turned back to me with a smile.

"No offense, but you look like hell," he said.

"Thanks," I muttered, waving him at the couch. He sat and then so did I. "I didn't sleep too well last night. I had a lot to think about."

He nodded. "Make any decisions?"

I took a breath and looked around. There had been so much in my head, but I thought that I had decided. There was still that one lingering doubt, but there was nothing I could do about that, and I had the rest of my life to think about. More than just this one moment.

"Yeah, I think I have," I began. "I want—"

Another knock on the door interrupted me. I looked at the door and then at him, with absolutely no clue who that could be. Even in Adelheid, door-to-door sales kept mostly to daylight hours, and I wasn't expecting anyone. I got up and moved to it, looking through the window again. My eyes flew open, and I nearly choked. I swallowed my tongue and gave a 'one moment' gesture to Gabe as I slipped out the door, opening it while trying to keep him from seeing outside while trying to not look like that's what I was doing.

"What are you doing here?" I all but hissed at Chance as he stood on my damn doorstep.

"I can't do it," he declared. "I can't let you go. I thought I could. I thought it was casual and I could just say good-bye, but I can't. I fucking can't. You're too much part of me, and I can't let you leave and go marry some fucking dog."

"*I'm* some fucking dog, Chance," I snapped, even though I knew that wasn't the point.

He gave me a look that said he thought the same thing. "I can't do it, Madison," he said. Raking his hands through his hair, he looked off to the side and then frowned as if noticing Gabe's truck for the first time. "Is he fucking here?" he demanded.

I panicked. "Chance!" I put my hands against his chest as he made for the door. I couldn't really hold him back, though. He had over a hundred pounds on me. He moved around me and blew through the door, me rushing after him. I saw Gabe already on his feet, and the wolf's 6'2" came a lot closer to the boxer's size. Gabe was a bit thicker, too.

"What the fuck you think you're doing, stealing another man's woman?" Chance raged.

Gabe was unmoved. As an alpha, he would hardly be the type to be cowed by a show of temper, even by a heavyweight. "Last I knew, Madison was her own woman," he replied evenly, although I could see the challenge in his intense eyes.

How was this happening? For a moment, I kind of just stood and watched in horror as the two of them postured without actually doing much. It was auras. I had never been the type of girl who wanted men to fight over her, and I certainly didn't want that now! My simple answers suddenly seemed to go to hell.

"Of course she's her own woman, but one who happened to be with me, and now suddenly, out of nowhere, there's you?" Chance returned, staring hard down at Gabe. The 'eye each other' thing that boxers did had no effect whatsoever.

"She makes her own decisions. Besides, I thought you two were *casual*. So, what right do you think you have to show up on her door acting like a possessive ass?" He had managed to put so much disdain on the word 'casual' that I thought Chance might actually try to hit him.

"I have every right to fucking show up," Chance snapped. "*I love her!*"

"Don't act like you're the only one here who cares for her," Gabe retorted.

I thought I saw his shoulder shift like he would throw a punch. That broke the ice around my feet, and I dove between them, putting my back to Gabriel's chest and both of my hands on Chance's, leveraging between them. "Stop it!" I shouted as loud as I could. I felt them almost ignoring me to try to get to each other. "*STOP IT!*" I shrieked.

They stopped pushing toward one another and looked at me. I moved out, looking at them both and realizing that they were looking at me for an answer.

An answer I didn't have. I loved Chance, but I cared

about Gabe and I loved the future being with him would give me. How did one choose between those?

I panicked.

Never in my life had I expected to deal with a situation like this, and I had honestly never wanted to. Looking between them and feeling the weight of expectations, the waiting, I felt like I was suffocating. I couldn't choose.

I bolted. Shamefully, I ran. I couldn't handle the moment and ran out the still-open door into the night.

❰O❱

It wasn't the smartest move I had ever made, and that didn't fully dawn on me until it was too late. Adrenaline kept me going longer than was good for the rest of me, and it wasn't until I was deep into the forest behind the house that I realized it was the middle of the night in March in New England and I had bare feet with pajama pants and a T-shirt.

When I finally got myself to stop, I realized that my feet hurt like hell. I must have cut them up on the foliage. I was also freezing, chattering instantly. I started walking back while thinking it through. And because this was my luck, just as I decided that wolf form would be better, the stupidest damn thing happened.

I stepped in a hole.

It was pretty deep and bracketed by roots. I fell forward, and my weight jerked my foot, breaking my ankle. Yes, I broke my damn ankle. I screamed in pain, but there was no one around to hear me. It took me five minutes to get my foot out of that hole and in every instant, I was sure that I did more damage to it in the process.

Flopping back on the cold ground, I cried. I sobbed. I tried to shift, but the pain kept distracting the process.

Then the sky rumbled, and a freak spring thunderstorm

rolled over my head.

My sobs turned to laughing, because what the fuck else could go wrong?

"Are you kidding me?" I screamed at the sky as it started to rain. The water was frigid and stung me with every drop. It occurred to me that my one dumb decision might, in fact, be the death of me. I couldn't shift, and I might freeze to death before my preternatural healing could catch up with me.

I didn't want to die. I was just dreaming about a future...

❨○❩

Rolling over onto my stomach, I pushed myself up on my hands and knees. I tried to keep the bad ankle from the ground, but it was very hard to do with such uneven ground. Every time that ankle lowered, it hit a root or something and I screamed again. The pain weakened me, and the rain kept its deluge. In fact, it seemed to get stronger.

The chill sunk into my body and made every movement like I was in a swimming pool of molasses. I kept moving, but it got harder and harder. I kept crying, because I couldn't stop. I didn't want to die, but I knew I was a long way from the house, and I could barely see. Was I even going the right way?

I kept moving. Until I couldn't anymore, then I collapsed and folded myself into a ball. And wept until it all went dark.

March 19th

The world shifted in and out. My eyes opened slightly when I felt a nose pressing against me. I looked feebly and saw a giant tiger head nudging my face. Beyond him was a giant black wolf. I thought I was hallucinating, fading back out and then in.

"Fuck, is she dead?"

"I don't think so, but she's pretty damn close."

I didn't know how I had woken up. At first, I thought that maybe I was dead and this was the afterlife, but the afterlife would probably hurt less. I hurt like hell. Everything hurt. I could barely move, and yet somehow I was moving. I started crying again, but it felt like no tears were actually coming.

"She's awake," the first voice said. Now I recognized it as Chance's voice. "You have to take her for a minute. Fuck, it's cold."

I felt myself shift through the air and realized that I was being carried. I felt bare skin next to my arms and cheek, and weakly, my brain put the pieces together.

They had searched, together, for me in animal form. And now two naked men were carrying my home.

It was almost too much, and I faded out again.

When next I opened my eyes, I was on my own couch and surrounded by blankets. I saw that my head was on someone's lap. When I looked up and saw that Gabe was on the phone, half-dressed and looking panicked, I knew I was on Chance.

"We found her in the woods... Yeah, she was out there for hours... Werewolf... She's been in and out of consciousness... Thank you." He stuffed his phone in his pocket and came to kneel in front of me, brushing still-freezing hair off my forehead. He looked up as he spoke. Now I could hear his teeth chattering slightly as he talked. "They're on their way." His expression became wry. "I know, I know. But I don't think either of us can drive."

I could feel my fingers and toes, but the tingling was agony. I shuddered and felt like crying, but I thought my tears were frozen. Everything else hurt in other ways, and I just wanted to burrow into the blankets until it was all over, or I died. At that point, I wasn't sure I cared which anymore.

I passed out again.

The next time I woke, I was in the hospital. I had an IV in my arm and four warm blankets on top of me. The painful tingling had stopped, but I still felt like something that had been hit by a tractor trailer and left by the side of the highway. Looking to my left, I saw Gabe sitting in the chair next to my bed. His arms were folded on the edge of the mattress and his head was on them. I could hear him sleeping.

To my right, I saw Chance stretched out on the other bed. The odd flickering thought in my brain hoped it had been empty before and he hadn't evicted someone.

They were both there. Something warm and painful opened in the center of my chest. I reached out and lightly touched the top of Gabe's head. He sat up, clearly startled, but then realized what had happened and his body relaxed. He took my hand in both of his. "Madison," he said with relief, briefly pressing his forehead against our clasped hands. "You scared the shit out of us." He lifted his head and called, "Chance, she's awake."

At the sound of Gabe's voice, Chance woke up and seemed to be on my other side in an instant, kissing the top of my head. "Don't do that again, sugar," he whispered.

"It was hardly a plan," I said weakly. "Am...I okay?"

"Once they got your warm, your preter healing took care of the leg. Now they're just making sure everything is okay. They say you'll go home tomorrow morning. They're actually about to kick us out of here," Gabe said with a weak smile. "We've been harassing the doctors." I wanted to ask about the "we" part, but he stood. "Sleep now." He kissed my hand.

"Rest," Chance echoed, kissing my head again.

Then they walked out together.

I stared after them, wondering if the cold had damaged my brain. Or if I was hallucinating. Either way, I fell back asleep and let my body finish healing.

March 20th

I was just finishing getting dressed when the boys walked into the hospital room. Someone had left me some clothes. I guessed it was Gabe, since it seemed more his style to remember something like that. The doctors had cleared me to leave, saying I had no permanent damage from my "rather reckless behavior," as they put it. I was calling it my "really dumb-ass move." It worked either way.

They came in together, just like they had left together. I still wasn't sure what to make of that. I smiled at both of them, though.

"My heroes," I said warmly, and with no small amount of embarrassment. "I am so sorry. I would say I don't know what I was thinking, but it's pretty damn obvious that I wasn't thinking at all. I just kinda freaked out."

Chance had his hands in his pockets and the good grace to join me in my embarrassment. "Yeah, well, your dumb-as-fuck boyfriend didn't help matters."

Somehow, hearing him call himself my boyfriend stung. I didn't know what was what anymore, and I didn't know what I was going to do. I figured I could at least heal before being faced with all that insanity.

"I don't suppose I did either," Gabe added, with some ruefulness although less of the embarrassment that Chance and I had. "He and I have had plenty of time to talk about that while worrying our asses off about you."

I sat on the edge of the bed, feeling like there was something coming. I felt a pit open up in the middle of my stomach as I tried to jump ahead of the game and figure out what it was. There suddenly seemed to be a lot less air in my lungs, although I wasn't entirely sure what I thought was about to happen...except that I knew I was going to lose one of them.

"We had a lot of time to talk," Chance said. He sat on the edge of the bed next to me while Gabe pulled up a chair. "It's amazing how much time you can fit in to think while going out of your damn head."

"Okay..." I said slowly, nervously.

"We think we might have a solution to the problem that made you go flying out of the house," Gabe said. He was definitely the grownup here. "It won't be easy, but it might be worth a try. We realized, when we both thought we were going to lose you, that we each love you...each in our own ways."

When he didn't go on, I thought my head might explode. "Well... What?" I prompted almost desperately.

Gabe looked past me to Chance, who cleared his throat. "Well, you and I keep keepin' on like we have been. We're still us, and when we're in the same town, we hook up." I looked at him with my brows drawing in. He looked at Gabe, and I grew more agitated by the moment as I turned back to the wolf.

"And you marry me and be pack alpha," he said. "Kind of a...closed open relationship. People do it, you know."

"Both?" I asked, feeling like I hadn't heard them right. The void in my stomach turned into a knot in my throat. The part of me force-fed romantic comedies since I was a girl said that this idea was wrong, but then... I was a fucking werewolf. I'd been thumbing my nose at contemporary society by existing, so why stop now? Once I thought about it, I recalled I had known people who did that kind of relationship, but I hadn't ever thought about it for myself. "Could...you two manage that? You are both kinda...dominant."

"Yeah, well," Chance began with a laugh. "We'll see how it goes. We're willing to try, though. It could work out great."

"I want you as my alpha," Gabe said. "I think you're just what the pack needs. It'll work best, for the laws of the pack and the laws of man, if we're married. But married can be whatever we want it to be."

I bit my lip and looked between them. I felt like someone shouldn't be this spoiled, but it was our lives, right?

"I think we should try," I said softly. "I don't want to lose either of you, or what I have with either of you."

"Then we'll try," Gabe said, taking my hand. "And see what comes."

"Like always, babe," Chance said, kissing my head. "We're just happy you're alive."

So was I.

❨O❩

The pack had once again gathered in the clearing. The moon was waned from its full state, but it was still bright enough to shine clearly upon us all. Ceremony was a little less alluring than bloodlust apparently since the crowd was not quite as large as the full moon fight had been, but that was okay.

Dozens of wolves surrounded the clearing again, plus several vampires in the shadows and one tiger alongside us. Everyone wondered, you could tell, but no one asked. He was the honored guest of the pack alphas, so who was really going to argue? Certainly not to our faces. When the rest of us howled, he roared. It was totally out of place and yet somehow, in my head and in my heart, it fit perfectly.

Before the pack, and Chance, Gabriel and I stood before each other in wolf form. We pressed our heads together and then rubbed necks. We did this on both sides, before laying down side by side.

After a moment, we stood and shifted back to our human forms. We stood before each other and took hands, reciting the vows that alpha mates had been reciting to each other for ages. There would be a human style wedding later, for legal reasons, but to the pack, this was the one that mattered. We made the vows and the pack howled, with its one roar amongst the lot.

When it was over, they all went their separate ways and left us alone in the clearing. The wolves disappeared, but the one tiger remained. And when they were all gone, he shifted back to his human form and walked up to us.

"Tigers ain't got shit like this," he quipped, back to his Chance Landry self. But he was smiling. "It was kinda nice, though. And you know, didn't feel nearly as fucking weird as I thought it would. Funny thing, that."

I laughed, unable to believe what was laying before me. My mirth faded for a moment. "You know if people find out about this, they're probably gonna say some awful things. Especially about me."

Chance reached out and took my hand. "When we ever care what dumb-ass things dumb-ass people gotta say about us, huh? I hear all kinds of shit while moving on the circuit, but I don't let it get to me. Don't let it get to you either."

Gabe took my other hand. "Yes, what he said." Then he smiled.

The two of them smiling at me brought my smile back. Life was going to get weird, but I had this feeling deep down that it would be okay. Maybe I was never meant to live a life like everyone else, but that was okay too.

The number three had become very important. It had become a blessing, and I was going to keep it that way.

If you want to know more about the town of Adelheid, the people who live in it, and the lore I chose to use when writing these preternatural species, you can check out my series wiki at wiki.authorkbthorne.com.

About the Author

Born a Connecticut Yankee in nobody's court, K. B. Thorne grew up to brave snow and talk fast.

She started reading when she was three and never looked back, soon frequently falling asleep with a book under her cheek. At eleven, she discovered *Night Mare* by Piers Anthony and entered the world of grown-up fantasy fiction. As you can guess, it was all over from there. She started writing at fourteen, then met vampires as a teenager and the concept for what would become Adelheid (now the Blood Rights Series) was soon born. Mia Darien followed a few years later, and the books were released.

However, K. B. is also a third-generation Trekkie. Somewhere in a vault at Paramount is a very angry letter written by her grandmother when *Star Trek: The Original Series* was cancelled, so sci-fi is in the blood too. Alongside a love of love and an adoration for her first love of epic fantasy.

K. B. Thorne is the evolution of Mia Darien after years of learning and living. She has taken both of those things to become a smarter, better writer with a fresh new face and take on the literary world. Thorne writes the urban fantasy, fantasy and sci-fi, while Sadie Johnston writes the romance.

These days, when she's not desperately trying to find time to write, she works as a freelance editor/cover artist/formatter and happily lives her unconventional life alongside her very own Named Man of the North and their mini-tank. (Who is, you know, their son.)

You can find K. B. at authorkbthorne.com!

OTHER BOOKS BY K. B. THORNE

Writing as K. B. Thorne
Blood Rights Series

Bad Blood
Blood and Thunder
Blood Moon
Written in Blood
Bloodshot
First Blood
Out for Blood
New Blood
Flesh and Blood

Out for Blood Series
Bones & Blood

Bellator (Anthology)
Good Things (Anthology)
Ashes to Sunrise (Anthology)
The Shape of Tomorrow (Anthology)
Born of Defiance (Anthology)

Writing as Sadie Johnston (Romance)
Beauty
Help Wanted (with Viola Dawn)
Threnody (with Alastair Malone)
Here, Kitty Kitty (Anthology)
Amor Vincit Omnia (Anthology)
Second Chances (Anthology)